D1095250

THE PIPER'S PROMISE

➤ Also in the SISTERS EVER AFTER series ◄

Thornwood
Glass Slippers

⇒ SISTERS EVER AFTER ⇐

THE PIPER'S PROMISE

Leah Cypess

DELACORTE PRESS

Text copyright © 2023 by Leah Cypess
Jacket art copyright © 2023 by Maxine Vee

All rights reserved. Published in the United States by Delacorte Press, an imprint of
Random House Children's Books, a division of Penguin Random House LLC, New York.

Delacorte Press is a registered trademark and the colophon
is a trademark of Penguin Random House LLC.

Visit us on the Web! rhcbooks.com

Educators and librarians, for a variety of teaching tools,
visit us at RHTeachersLibrarians.com

Library of Congress Cataloging-in-Publication Data
Names: Cypess, Leah, author.
Title: The piper's promise / Leah Cypess.
Other titles: Pied Piper of Hamelin. English.
Description: First edition. | New York : Delacorte Press, [2023] |
Series: Sisters ever after ; book 3 | Audience: Ages 10 and up. |
Summary: "The Pied Piper's little sister Clare is determined to uncover the truth
behind her brother's seemingly cruel actions"—Provided by publisher.
Identifiers: LCCN 2021058636 (print) | LCCN 2021058637 (ebook) |
ISBN 978-0-593-17891-1 (hardcover) | ISBN 978-0-593-17893-5 (ebook) |
Subjects: CYAC: Brothers and sisters—Fiction. | Fairies—Fiction. |
Characters in literature—Fiction.
Classification: LCC PZ7.C9972 Pi 2023 (print) | LCC PZ7.C9972 (ebook) | DDC [Fic]—dc23

The text of this book is set in 12.5-point Golden Cockerel ITC Std.
Interior design by Carol Ly

Printed in the United States of America
1st Printing
First Edition

To David

⇛ PROLOGUE ⇚

I know what you've heard about my brother. That he's evil. That he's a liar and a thief. That he has terrible taste in clothing.

That he played his magic pipe and stole the children of Hamelin, leading them to a faraway land where their parents couldn't follow.

All those things are sort of true, but they're also not true. Not the way you think they are.

The story of the Pied Piper did happen the way you heard it. The town of Hamelin was infested with rats until a stranger in colorful clothes offered to take care of the problem. His price was high, but the mayor was desperate and agreed.

So the boy took out his pipe and played it, and all the rats were drawn to the sound. He led them to the river and then *into* the river, and they followed the music to their deaths.

"Sorry!" the mayor said the next day. "Your fee is criminally high. But since I'm so glad to be rid of the rats, I won't throw you in jail. I'll simply pay you a *fair* price and send you on your way."

He probably thought he was so clever. After all, it wasn't as if the piper could bring the rats back.

And the piper didn't. He waited until the next morning, and then he played a different tune on his pipe. This time, it wasn't rats who came streaming to the music. It was the town's children, dancing and laughing, pushing and fighting each other in their eagerness to be first.

The Pied Piper led them down the road from Hamelin and right into the side of the mountain, and their parents never saw them again.

That's how the story ends in every version I've heard. Some mention a few children who got left behind because they were deaf or blind or had trouble walking. Others don't. All agree, however, that the people of Hamelin lost their children forever because they refused to pay the piper.

And that's how the story *should* end. That's the lesson people need to learn: don't try to cheat one of the fae. It never ends well.

But you haven't heard about me, have you?

In the story your parents tell, my brother is the

villain and the townspeople his innocent victims. Your parents are smart. There's a good reason they don't tell you about me.

Because once I walked into Hamelin, the story got a lot more complicated.

1

The parents were grieving, and their grief was terrible to bear. Both because of the depth and sharpness of their sadness, and because I knew that if anything horrible ever happened to me or Tom, our mother would never grieve for us that way.

I wasn't sure she would grieve for us at all.

Love is a burden, Tom told me once, that time when I almost got eaten by a sea serpent and our mother laughed as she told the fae court about it. Tom had been the one to save me, and then to hold me tight as I coughed up water. But when I came to him sobbing over our mother's lack of caring, he had pressed his lips together impatiently. *The other side of love is pain.*

I saw that pain now as I walked through the shabby gray streets of Hamelin. It leaked from every window in this small, dusty town, glared from every tear-streaked face that watched me pass.

I understood that grief. For weeks now, I had been missing my brother—a constant, empty ache under my heart. I knew how powerful that anguish was, because it had led me to do the unthinkable: to leave the Realms, by myself, and come to the human world to find him.

And I would find him. I *would*. No matter what had happened to him, no matter what he had done, I would find him and we would be together again.

But I had never imagined that I was going to find *this*. Not my brother, but the pain he had left behind. And the only thing that made it bearable was the determination I clung to: *I can fix this.*

I didn't know for sure if that was true. But I forced myself to believe it, because there was no other way I could have made it down that eerily silent street, up the stairs of the grandest house in town, and into the mayor's office.

The mayor's "office" was actually the front room of his house, which says a lot about how often Hamelin's yearly elections resulted in a change of mayor. Mayor Herman, I'd been told, had been the mayor for over twenty years. It would probably help if someone occasionally ran *against* him, but since no one ever did, the ballots generally had two choices: *Herman Jeremson* and *Somebody Else, If We Can Find Someone Qualified and Willing,*

Which Is Unlikely. Written on the ballot, just like that—I'd seen one stuck under a grimy well stone, left over from the last election.

Not the most democratic of places, Hamelin. Not that it would have helped much if it had been.

The mayor's office reeked of stale tobacco, and his face shone with sweat. He sat upright in his brown leather chair, brow furrowed, as if he was in control of the situation. But I, of all people, could recognize tightly controlled fear. *He* had been the one who hired my brother as a ratcatcher. *He* had been the one who refused to pay the exorbitant fee. Any moment now, the people's grief would turn into anger, and they would remember who was responsible for the tragedy that had overtaken their town.

They would be wrong. My brother had come for their children, and he would have found a way to take them even if Hamelin had a smart and honest mayor.

But nobody knew that except me. And I certainly wasn't about to tell Mayor Herman.

The mayor looked up as I entered. He drew in his breath, and I wondered if he recognized something in me that reminded him of Tom. If he was remembering the last time a lanky, dark-haired child had walked into his office and offered to solve his problems.

I hoped not. But I had to be careful, just in case.

"Mayor Herman," I said, and curtsied. His eyes widened in astonishment, from which I gathered that it was not customary to curtsy to mayors. Human etiquette rules were so confusing. "I am here to help you get Hamelin's children back."

"Are you?" He sat back, regarding me with sharp blue eyes. "And what payment will you ask in return?"

I had expected either joy or disbelief. I knew then that something was wrong, but I couldn't think fast enough to change my plan. "No payment. I only want to make sure the children are unharmed. Can you tell me which way they went?"

The mayor leaned forward as if listening. But his eyes flicked to the door behind me.

Too late, I realized what was happening.

I turned, but not fast enough. Two men burst into the room. One had a bristling black beard that stuck straight out from his chin, the other a large, furry mustache that looked like it had been glued crookedly to his face. Before I could move, the man with the mustache had my arms pinned behind my back. I tried to twist free, but the bearded man grabbed my right arm and snapped a thick iron band around my wrist.

After that, the only thing I could do was scream.

I did scream, at the top of my lungs. Of course, no

one came to help me. The townspeople were not par-
tial to mysterious strangers right now.

The bearded man stepped away from me. "Should I
slap her," he asked, "to shut her up?"

He sounded like he really wanted to. I gulped, silencing myself.

"Good girl," the mayor said. He came out from behind his desk and stood in front of me. The mustached
man still had my arms pinned behind me and the
bearded one glowered at me from beside the mayor.
Each was nearly twice my height, but the mayor still
made sure to leave several yards between him and me.

It was nice to have a reputation.

It would have been even nicer if I deserved that reputation.

I snarled at the mayor. He flinched, then puffed his
chest out. Too late; I had seen the flinch, and so had his
hairy-faced henchmen.

"You *will* get us our children back," he said. "And
I'll give you nothing in return except your worth-
less life."

From the way the bearded man looked at him sideways, I knew the mayor had no intention of giving me
that, either.

"Tell us where they are," the mayor said.

"I don't know!" I gasped. The iron band on my wrist hurt—not as much as it would have if I was fully fae, but still, it felt like hives were breaking out wherever it touched my skin. "I swear, I don't know! That's why I came here, so you could tell me which way they went."

The bearded man strode forward and struck me in the face, so hard my head snapped to one side.

The mayor opened his mouth as if to object, then closed it. He looked very proper in his fine dark clothes, his trim beard a distinguished blend of gray and white. But when the man raised his hand again, Mayor Herman didn't tell him to stop.

"Where did you take them?" he demanded.

"I didn't take them anywhere! Do I *look* like the Pied Piper to you?"

Which was a foolish question. Of course I did.

I had made a mistake, coming here. I had thought I understood humans better than I did. Tom had warned me about exactly that—*Just because we were born human, doesn't mean we know how to think like them. We've lived our whole lives among the fae.* I should have paid more attention.

To the fae, Tom and I were nearly identical. They got us mixed up constantly. But humans could tell us apart easily—even Anna, who had trouble telling most people apart. I had once asked her how she did it, and she had burst into laughter and said, "Are you joking? He's several handsbreadth taller than you!"

But apparently, even to humans, Tom and I looked similar. We *were* brother and sister. Thin, dark-haired, and dark-eyed, with bony jaws and jutting cheekbones.

"I'm not the piper!" I shouted. "I'm not the one who stole your children!"

"Give us a straight answer," the man behind me growled.

The mayor motioned him into silence. "Where did you and your brother take our children?"

"I didn't," I said. "It was just him." After a too-long pause, I added, "I'm sorry."

"I've heard," the mayor said, "that the fae can't lie. But if you're human, then you'd be perfectly capable of lying, wouldn't you?"

The fae work very hard at spreading that rumor. They're actually quite good at lying. And I, personally, am *very* good at lying.

But as it happened, I was telling the truth. How to convince the mayor of that, though?

"My brother and I have spent most of our lives in the Faerie Realms," I said. "The magic of their land has seeped into us—through our skin, our breath, our food. It has made us somewhat fae, even though we were born fully human."

"What does that mean?"

"It means," I said, "that I can lie, but it would cause me great pain. I don't lie unless I have a good reason to. And I'm not lying now."

Mayor Herman clasped his hands behind his back and stepped forward diagonally—giving the impression that he was approaching me, while in reality keeping the same distance between us. "Say I believe you. Why did your brother take them?"

"I don't know why he took them." My skin had adjusted somewhat to the iron band, so the pain had become a dull, constant itch. It was still distracting, but not quite as much as having my arms held behind my back. "I haven't seen him in months."

"Are the children—" His voice caught. "Are they alive?"

I didn't know the answer to that. I didn't want to think Tom would actually let innocent children die. Then again, I was having trouble thinking about what he was doing. My mind kept shuddering back from it, as if ignoring it might make it not true.

I gave the mayor an answer anyhow. "They're alive. I'm sure he hasn't hurt them."

The mayor gave me an incredulous look. From his perspective, I suppose, Tom had already hurt them.

"If you don't know why he took them," the mayor said, "and you don't know where they are, how are you planning to get them back?"

"If that's really what you're planning," the bearded man added. This time, he ignored the mayor's silencing gesture. He was, I could tell, going to hit me again soon, whether the mayor liked it or not.

"I'll follow him," I said. "I can go wherever he can. If you show me which way he took the children, I'll track him down."

"And when you *do* catch up to your brother," the man with the mustache cut in, tightening his grip on my arms, "how do you plan to get the children away from him?"

"I know which spell he used," I said. "All I need to do is find him and I can break it."

Like I said: I'm *very* good at lying.

The truth was, the main thing I wanted from Tom was answers. He probably had a good reason for what he had done; for all I knew, he was saving the children, not stealing them. Once he explained everything to me, I might even end up helping him.

The mayor definitely didn't need to know that. So I said nothing else until he nodded abruptly and gestured at the man with the mustache.

My wrists were released so suddenly that I stumbled forward. I managed not to fall or to whimper from the pain in my shoulders. I straightened.

"Tell me which way he went," I said.

The mayor pressed his lips together. I could see that he still didn't trust me; he wasn't quite as foolish as I had assumed. Which shouldn't have surprised me. After all, if the mayor was really such a fool, how had he managed to stay mayor for almost twenty years now?

I knew what Tom would have said to that: *Because humans are fools, too.* Tom had a habit of forgetting that we were also human.

In the end, though, it didn't matter how smart the mayor was. I was the only person offering him a solution to his terrible situation. What could he do but take it?

Which was probably exactly what he had thought when Tom came to him the first time.

"When you come back with them," he said, "we'll pay you what we owe your brother."

"Sure," I agreed. Why not?

"And we'll take off the iron band."

From the way the mayor smiled, I knew my reaction had been visible. I forced my voice to stay even. "You need to take it off *now*. I can't work magic with iron on me. I won't be able to break the spell."

"That's why I'll come with you." He held up one hand. A tiny key dangled from it, swinging lightly back and forth. "When we catch up to the children, I'll take the band off."

If I showed panic, I was done. I forced myself steady, a maneuver that was very familiar to me. The fae liked to play with human children—to taunt and tease and frighten us—and their carelessness often led to human deaths. But if you showed no reaction, if you were a boring plaything, they would usually leave you alone.

So I had become very good at hiding fear. But usually Tom was right beside me, pretending along with me. He was the one who had taught me how to do it. I had never realized how much of my technique was actually just copying him.

I thought of how he would act now: calm, sure, rakish. I put a bit of his cockiness into my voice. "It's an excellent idea. But it won't work. No adult human can pass into the Faerie Realms. I couldn't take you with me even if I wanted to."

The mayor stepped back, looking lost. The bearded man stepped forward, hand swinging forward.

"Then take me," a voice said from the doorway.

2

The girl in the doorway was tall, with white-gold hair, pale blue eyes, and a vague expression on her face that made her look less alert than she really was.

My heart sank. But I kept up my pretense of confidence. "Hello, Anna."

"Clare," she responded. She held her long, thin white cane in front of her, not quite resting it on the ground. "I guess you weren't expecting to see me here?"

I fought not to react, in case she was able to make out my expression. I was never quite sure how much Anna could see. She was partially blind—she had been born that way, and it was something no spectacles could fix. But even though she couldn't recognize most people unless they were right in front of her, she had proved herself very able to read my moods.

Most people who didn't know her assumed she couldn't see anything. She let them think so—it was too tiresome to keep explaining otherwise, she had told me once. But I always thought she preferred to let people underestimate how much she noticed, rather than have them assume she saw more than she did.

Behind me, the mayor drew in a strangled breath. "Anna," he said, his voice rising in shock. "What are you doing here?"

Anna didn't glance at him. She walked into the room, sweeping her cane ahead of her. Her drab brown dress was rumpled and sweat-stained, and her hair floated in disheveled strands around her face. She stopped directly in front of me.

"You're looking well," she said. Anna had a beautiful voice; it always sounded like she was on the verge of singing, even when her words were short and angry.

"You *know* her?" the mayor spluttered.

It wasn't clear which of us he was speaking to. But it was Anna who answered. "Oh yes. We used to be good friends."

Used to be. Something inside me shriveled.

"When?" the mayor demanded.

A good question. It had been about half a year in the Realms, but it could have been any amount of time here. Anna didn't look that different, though; I guessed she was still thirteen, fourteen at most. So it hadn't been that long for her, either.

"She says she can bring the children back," the man with the mustache interrupted. His voice was hoarse, and a bit of his desperation slipped through. "Can she do it?"

Anna cocked her head. Her hair had been cut short since I'd last seen her; its tangled edges swayed about her chin, lit into glimmering strands by the sunlight streaming through the windows. "Maybe."

"Maybe," the bearded man said, "isn't good enough."

"I doubt she knows herself whether she can do it," Anna said. "But I believe she'll try her hardest."

The mayor let out a breath. "So she can be trusted?"

"Oh no," Anna said. "Definitely not."

I felt like I was going to cry, and I focused on holding the tears in. I made myself into a hot brick wall, a cool rush of water, a wide-eyed statue. All the tricks I had spent my childhood practicing. Nothing amused the fae as much as human tears.

I imagined that Tom was there, holding my hand. Sometimes, when he saw that I was losing the battle with tears, he would dig his fingernails into my knuckles sharply enough for the pain to distract me.

"She was raised by the fae," Anna said. "She and her brother both. Back before the Pact, the fae used to take children all the time."

"But the Pact between humans and the fae was struck more than a hundred years ago," the mayor protested. "That girl can't be older than eleven, and her brother was, what—sixteen? Seventeen?"

"Time passes differently in the Faerie Realms," I said, turning slightly so I could see both the mayor and Anna. I had won my battle with the tears, and I didn't feel like letting Anna tell my story for me. "Sometimes faster, sometimes slower. In our case, it was slower. Eight years passed for my brother and me while we lived in the Realms, but over a hundred here, like you said. When I finally came back a few weeks ago, it was to find that my parents were long dead."

I had tried to find my parents at first—and then, to at least find out something about them. I didn't remember them, but Tom had shared some of his memories with me, and I'd grown up dreaming about the human mother who actually cared about me. But nobody knew anything about a couple who had lost their children some unspecified number of years ago—and worse than that, nobody believed me. It had been so long since the Pact was struck, since the faeries had agreed to stay in their own realm and stop causing trouble in the human world. No one living now had ever seen a faerie. Many had stopped believing in faeries altogether.

"I'm sorry," the mayor said. "That must have been terrible. But taking our children won't change what happened to you and your brother."

"I know," I said. "I don't—I can't understand why my brother would do this." There was enough truth in that to make my voice wobble. *He didn't do it*, I told myself fiercely. *He didn't.* Once I found him, he would explain what had really happened, and I would feel silly for ever suspecting him. I firmed up my voice. "But I'll fix it. I'll bring your children back. I promise."

The bearded man raised his hand again, but the mayor motioned for him to stop. To my relief, he did, though he gave me a look that promised, *Later.*

"Why should I believe you?" the mayor said.

"I didn't have to come here," I pointed out. "And I'm not asking you for anything. Why would I be in Hamelin if not to help you?"

"I don't know," the mayor said. "I don't understand the faes' tricksy ways."

That was for sure—I had lived with the fae all my life, and I still didn't understand their ways—but my opinion of the mayor inched higher. You have to be *quite* smart to understand that there's something you're not smart enough to understand.

"I told you," I said. "I'm not fae."

Which was only half a lie. I had been just three years

old when I first stumbled into the Realms. I had never known any manners but those of the fae. Tom and I had eaten fae food and spent time with fae guardians and always, always been surrounded by magic, seeping into our skins and shaping our minds. We might have been fully human when we entered the Realms, but we were, by now, more fae than human.

Or so I'd thought—until just this morning, when I heard what my brother had done to the children of Hamelin, and a purely human horror had twisted through me.

And here I was, setting off to save them. Because I couldn't bear the suffering of those children, even though I didn't know any of them. It was the most human thing I could imagine doing.

If anyone in the Realms ever found out about it, they would mock me forever.

"You don't have to trust her," Anna said, folding her arms across her chest. "I'll go with her to make sure she keeps her promise."

"Absolutely not," the mayor said. "It's too dangerous. I still don't understand how the two of you even met."

"I'll tell you later," Anna said.

"You'll tell me *now*, because you're not going any-where with that creature. I forbid it."

Anna turned and squinted at him, which was when

I realized that she had avoided facing him until now. A memory flashed through me, something Anna had told me once while we floated on a crystal lake, watching mermaids show off their acrobatics: *I always felt trapped before I came here. It's not easy being the mayor's daughter.*

"You can't forbid me," Anna said. "Not this time. The town needs me to do this."

The mayor pressed his lips together. He started toward her, then hesitated and glanced at his two henchmen.

"It's our only chance to get the children back." Anna didn't look at the men, but it was clear she was speaking mostly to them.

The mayor looked at the man beside him and then at the man behind me, and his shoulders sagged.

It's not easy being the mayor's daughter. And then Anna had added: *But it has its advantages. I've learned from him how to get what I want.*

Anna looked nothing like her father. He was weighty and solid, while she looked like a stray gust of wind might carry her away. But when their eyes met, it was with the understanding of two people who know each other very well.

I recognized that look. I had shared it with Tom more than once.

"Be careful," the mayor said, and it was probably only his daughter—and me—who heard the defeat in his voice.

"Of course I will," Anna said. "Don't worry, Father. Clare will make sure I don't come to any harm."

I met her pale blue eyes. Her vague, off-center look disappeared as her gaze found mine and focused.

"Smile, Clare," she said. "This might even be fun."

3

The town provisioned us well, with water bags and two packs full of travel bread, and the townspeople gathered to see us off. We left from the town square, which was a large, non-square space in which cracked gray cobblestones struggled against the encroachment of grass and weeds. (The grass and weeds were winning.) A couple of stone basins filled with nothing but dirt bordered the space. In the center was a raised stone circle that looked like it had been meant to hold a statue but was instead littered with pebbles. The mayor stood on that platform while he made a short speech, which consisted mostly of taking credit for what Anna and I were about to do.

"My own daughter will lead this mission," he finished. "She will face the fae trickster who took our children from us. Have hope, my good people. I will . . ." His voice broke, and it took him a dramatic moment to recompose himself. "I will get them back. I swear it. Even if it is the last thing I do."

The people listened without a murmur, their faces pale and weary, their clothes gray and brown.

This entire town was gray, brown, and dusty. In the Realms, everything was alive with color all the time—more colors than humans even knew existed. Once, at a banquet, I accidentally drank from an enchanted goblet, and magic had spread through me before I could control it. I had seen what the fae saw—not a dozen colors swirling through the night sky, but hundreds of colors, gorgeous unearthly hues that had no name, because humans couldn't see them and the fae didn't bother to name them.

I had been so entranced I lost control of the magic—humans couldn't handle that much—and after the resulting debacle, which involved several members of the court turning into frogs or swans, Tom and I had spent a few months in an underground grotto waiting for our mother to forget how I had embarrassed her.

"Go," the mayor said to us. "Go as quickly as you can. Anna . . ." His voice wavered. This time, I didn't think he was faking it. "Be safe. We are all counting on you."

Anna's snort as we turned to go was so tiny that I was probably the only one who heard it.

As we started down the street, a woman broke from

the crowd. She was tall and lanky, with frizzy red hair escaping from her brown kerchief. Before anyone could move to stop her, she pressed a piece of paper into my hands.

I instinctively reached for magic. But we weren't in the Realms, where magic filled the air, easily available for the taking. Its lack left me gasping in shock, as it always did, even after all these weeks in the human world living without it.

But the woman wasn't attacking me. She stepped back, leaving me holding the paper.

"Bring them home," she said. Her voice was hoarse, and her eyes were nearly as red as her hair. "Please."

I looked down. I was holding a charcoal drawing of two children, a girl with two long braids and a boy with a shy, gap-toothed smile. Even in the rough sketch, the girl's eyes looked like they were dancing.

"Isabella!" the mayor roared, and his two hairy-faced henchmen surged forward. The woman backed away from me before they could reach her. Her eyes studied my face, like she was searching for something to give her hope.

"*Please,*" she said again. "They're my children. Bring them home."

I met her eyes and felt something in me break. I knew how she felt. I knew *exactly* how she felt, because I, too, was afraid that my brother would never come back to me.

"I'll find them," I said, and in that moment, I fully believed it. "I'll find your children and bring them back."

I folded the paper and put it in the pack the mayor had given me. Then I turned, not looking at the red-haired woman again, and followed Anna down the flat, dusty street.

Even though Anna was taller than me, her stride was slightly shorter than mine, so I had to adjust my pace to stay next to her. That forced me to walk slower than I wanted to. I kept expecting a ripe tomato, or something worse, to hit me in the back.

But nothing did. I guess the townspeople wanted their children back even more than they wanted to hurt me.

"He led them up the road that way," Anna said, once we were out of the village. The road wound ahead of us like a thin, jagged scar, disappearing into mountains that looked solid gray from a distance. The sun's rays were a hazy veil of white, making me squint and forcing Anna to look down—sunlight hurt her eyes. "Then he took them through the woods to the mountainside, dancing all the way. The children were dancing, I mean. Not Tom. He was just walking and playing his silver pipe."

I stopped walking. "His what?"

Anna nudged me in the side so hard I yelped. "Keep moving."

"But—"

"The townspeople know it was your brother who took their children, and they're still letting you walk away from here." She shook her head, as if she thought the townspeople had made a very bad decision. "I strongly suggest you *keep walking.*"

Something made a plopping sound beside me, and I jumped. But it wasn't a badly aimed tomato. It was just a frog.

All the same, I decided to take Anna's advice. I jerked forward, almost tripped over a loose stone, flailed frantically, and managed not to fall by stumbling several yards while windmilling my arms.

Anna's cane swept back and forth, tapping the ground lightly at the end of each arc. "That's not exactly what I had in mind."

I resisted the urge to look over my shoulder. Whatever hope I had given these people, it probably wasn't at its highest point right now.

Anna glanced at me sideways, and I wondered if I looked as different to her as she did to me. From this close, she could probably make out what I was wearing: an ordinary, drab human dress, which had once been light blue but had faded to a sort-of gray. I had traded for it weeks ago; it was far more practical than the shimmering green gown I'd crossed over in, but it also hung on me like a sack and got damp rather quickly when I sweated. Which I was doing now.

But all Anna said was, "You didn't know about his pipe?"

"I only heard a short version of the story, from a minstrel in another town."

Anna sighed. "Seems like it's a good thing I came along to help. What *do* you know about what happened?"

I lifted my chin. "The secrets of the fae are not mine to reveal."

"So . . . nothing?"

"A little more than nothing," I said. And then, reluctantly: "A *very* little more than nothing."

"Wonderful," Anna muttered. "Then why are you here?"

"I heard that Tom took the children away from this town." I deliberately said *took* rather than *stole*. "So I'm here to bring them back before anything bad happens to them."

"Why do you care what happens to them?" Anna kept her eyes on the road, squinting. "The other fae wouldn't care."

That was definitely true, though I wasn't sure how Anna knew it. I had kept her very far from the other fae during the month she'd spent with me in the Realms. "Tom and I aren't fae, exactly. We were born human. Living in the Realms has changed us—we've been raised to be fae—but we still know what it means to care."

Anna nodded, like I had just confirmed something she suspected. "Because you care about each other."

"Not just about each other." Something I had only realized this past month. Turned out, once you cared about one person, you couldn't keep it contained. Now I found myself caring about Anna's opinion of me, and the grief of that desperate woman in the village, and the fate of all those lost, confused children.

Being human must be *exhausting*.

"Speak for yourself." Anna stepped around a rut in the road. "Tom seems a lot more fae than you do."

"How would you know? You barely saw him."

Anna hesitated before replying. "I talked to him plenty, when he brought me back. I don't think there's much humanity left in him."

I kicked a pebble out of my way. "He's spent more time than me in the court, using magic, eating enchanted food. He had to; there was no one protecting *him*. So the

Realms have changed him more than they've changed me, but that doesn't mean he's really one of them."

"Right. And the fact that he stole children, does *that* mean he's one of them?"

"We don't know what he's doing," I snapped. "I know it *looks* like he stole them for no reason. But that's not necessarily . . ." The expression on Anna's face made me forget what I had been about to say. I finished, weakly, "We don't know the whole story."

"We know the part where he forced the children of my town to follow him into a mountain! We know the part where they've been missing for nearly an entire day, and no one knows whether they're alive or dead!"

I winced. Hopefully, time in the Realms was currently running slower than in the human world. Otherwise, if the children were there for more than a few days, there was no way they would all be alive when we found them.

"Come on, Anna. You say you know Tom." I hated the note of pleading in my voice, and tried to sound firmer. It came out angry, which was good enough. "You must know he wouldn't hurt anyone. There has to be something else going on."

Anna pressed her lips together. "I said I talked to him. I don't know him at all."

But you know me. Which would be a pointless, pathetic thing to say. So I didn't say it. Instead I said, "So the pipe was silver. Did it have a design of diamonds etched into its bottom side?"

"I don't know," Anna said. "I couldn't see that much detail."

"Right." I flushed. "Sorry."

"But I do know that its magic enchanted those who heard it. First the rats, then the children. They would have followed that music anywhere. Even if he had led them right into the river and drowned them, the way he did with the rats, they wouldn't have stopped."

There was a pang in her voice, more regret than fear. Her cane tapped the ground extra hard. I didn't have to ask why she hadn't been fast enough to follow the music all the way out of town along with the other children.

I sighed. "Then it's safe to assume it's what I think it is. The faerie queen's magic pipe."

Tom had stolen the *queen's* pipe. Was he mad? The faerie queen was notoriously cruel to those who crossed her. Her punishments were so bad that even other fae didn't like to speak of them—and that is *quite* bad.

Stealing a bunch of innocent human children—that was one thing. I didn't believe my brother would be so cruel, but I also had to admit that no one else at the fae court would see it that way. To the faeries, it would be a marvelous trick.

But if he had stolen the queen's pipe . . .

Then he had done it for a reason. The pipe was the only object the fae possessed that could reach across the borders between the Realms and the human world. It was invaluable.

I shivered despite the sunlight beating on my back. If Tom had stolen the pipe, he had done it for one reason only: to kidnap the children of Hamelin and take them to the Realms.

It wasn't a mistake. My brother truly had done this terrible thing.

And I had no idea why.

4

"I'll start at the beginning," Anna said. "With the rats."

I braced myself. The sun beat on the back of my neck, dust filled the air, and the band around my wrist was a constant nagging itch. But all those irritations were nothing compared to the dread I felt rising in me.

I had heard the story of the Pied Piper told by a minstrel to an enthralled crowd in a marketplace a few towns over. It was the sixth town I'd gone to after leaving the Realms, following clues and stories about a mysterious dark-haired boy in wildly colorful clothes. There was nothing solid, though, not until I heard the minstrel's tale: how just that morning, a faerie boy with a many-colored cloak had led all the children of Hamelin out of the town and into the side of a mountain. None of the children had been seen since.

I had known at once it was Tom. He loved that cloak and always took it with him when he left the Realms. A reminder of home, he'd told me once, to keep the colorlessness of the human world from weighing on him too heavily.

I had stood in the marketplace, holding a meat pie I'd purchased with enchanted coins, my stomach tightening into a hard, painful knot. I'd ended up throwing the meat pie away, which was too bad. The few bites I'd had were delicious.

The knot hadn't gone away over the next few hours, which I'd spent walking straight to Hamelin. Now it twisted even tighter as Anna spoke.

"It's been a bad year for rats," she said. "Lots of towns have been infested. But it was worst in Hamelin. I can't remember the last time I ate a loaf of bread that didn't have a rat bite in it. Friar Domenic says it's because the weather's been damp and the rats were able to breed and feed more than usual. Madam Elissa says it was a faerie curse."

"The friar's theory," I said, "sounds more likely."

The faeries used to call down curses on humans— they told gleeful stories about it all the time—but they were more inclined to put them to sleep for a hundred years or make jewels spill from their mouths than to call upon dull creatures like rats. Anyhow, since the Pact, the faeries had been forbidden to meddle in the human world.

"No one took Madam Elissa seriously," Anna agreed. "We tried cats, but the rats were fiercer than the cats. Sunny lost an ear, and Midnight limps now. We tried poison and traps, but the rats avoided both. Then your brother showed up. He promised he could get rid of the rats in exchange for a thousand gold guilders."

I stopped short. "A thousand guilders!"

Anna lifted her cane and used it to nudge me in the small of my back. "Could you find another way to express shock, please? At this rate we'll never get to the end of the road."

I started walking again. Yellow-brown fields scattered with tall trees stretched on either side of the road. Up ahead, the trees grew thicker, turning into a mass of green that climbed halfway up the mountain.

"We couldn't afford his fee, of course," Anna said. "But the rats were *horrible*. They would jump on the table and lick soup off our spoons. One morning my father put on his hat, and a nest of baby rats tumbled out."

I shuddered.

"Tom did what he promised. He told us all to stay indoors and stuff our ears with cotton, and then he played his pipe—at least, I assume he did—and led the rats into the river. When we came out they were gone, and they haven't returned."

"And then," I finished, "he asked for his payment." Payment he had no use for.

"Which my father couldn't give him." Anna sighed. "Tom showed up this morning playing a different tune on his pipe. Only the children could hear it, and our parents didn't realize what was happening until it was too late." Her voice caught. "For most of us."

Tap-tap went her cane.

"My father caught me," she said. "He held on to me while your brother led the other children into the side of the mountain, and the mountain closed behind them."

She said it smoothly—too smoothly. Something about her voice rang false. Why would the mayor be faster than any of the other parents? He certainly hadn't struck me as someone in excellent physical shape.

I had assumed Anna wasn't able to follow because her poor eyesight had slowed her down. Maybe that *was* the real reason, and she didn't want to say so. She was always worried that people would use her vision to restrict what she was allowed to do, the way her father did.

Anna chewed her lower lip, obviously concerned that I had sensed her lie. I decided to let it go. After all, she wasn't the only one lying. If Tom had stolen the children, I had no idea what I was going to do when I found him, or how I could get them back.

If they were still alive to be taken back.

No. Even if he took them, he wouldn't let anything bad happen to them. My brother might show a cruel face to the rest of the fae, but I knew who he really was: the brother who held me close when I cried, who taught me everything he had learned about the Realms, who always put protecting me above anything else.

He would listen to me. He *always* listened to me. I would remind him of who he truly was, and together we would fix this.

The road narrowed into little more than a trail, hard-packed dirt scattered with small stones. Around us the grass lengthened into cornstalks, and soon our path was lined by tall green and light brown fronds, with breaks between them that looked like narrow paths.

I glanced back. I could no longer see the town.

"All right," I said, stopping. "We're far enough out." I held out my arm.

Anna blinked. "Far enough out for what?"

"To take off the band."

She gave me a confused look. "We haven't found the children yet."

I dropped my arm, feeling like she had punched me in the stomach. "You can't be serious."

"You heard what my father said."

"Since when do *you* do what your father says?" I demanded. "If you were such an obedient daughter, we wouldn't even be friends."

Anna's lips formed a straight line. Behind her, the corn swayed lightly in the breeze. "Is that what we are?"

"Of course!" I found, to my horror, that I was on the verge of tears. *Never cry in front of them,* Tom's voice hissed in my mind. *I can't distract them once they see tears.* "We played and danced together. I showed you the mermaid lagoon! I gave you a ball gown made of feathers!"

She stepped back. I wondered if I was spitting. "And you thought that made us friends?"

"We were together a whole month!" It had been the best month of my life. Tom had been away on a mission for the queen, but instead of leaving me lonely, he'd brought me a friend. And we'd had so much fun that I hadn't had time to miss Tom or to be afraid of what the fae would do to me in his absence.

Anna shook her head. "It was only a few hours, Clare. When Tom brought me back home, my father hadn't even noticed I was gone."

"It was a few hours *here*." I waved a hand at the human

world around us. "But it was a whole month in the Realms, and that's what counts. Because that's where we *were*."

"It's not all that counted to *me*," Anna said. "I didn't know time would pass differently there. If you knew it would be just a few hours, why didn't you tell me?"

I opened my mouth, then closed it. The truth was, I hadn't known. Time moved differently in the Realms and in the human world, but not in a consistent way; sometimes it was slower, sometimes it was faster, sometimes it seemed exactly the same. For all I'd known, a decade might have passed in Hamelin during that month in the Realms.

"I thought my father would be worried sick about me," Anna went on. "I was sure that when I got back, he would lock me in my room for weeks. *If* I got back. I didn't know if you were ever going to let me out."

I frowned. "Why didn't you tell me?"

"I didn't know if you would care."

Anna was the first human—the first *full* human—I had gotten to know. There were humans scattered all around the Realms, people who had been there for hundreds of years; most had wandered in or been caught by spells or—in the most pathetic cases—had tried to bargain with the fae. They were objects of pity and mockery, and Tom and I steered clear of them. We didn't want to be thought of as *human*. It was the other fae whose attention we wanted, whose games and hunts we joined when they allowed us to.

We tried to fit in with the fae as much as possible, and the fae didn't pay much attention to the passage of time. Nor did they worry about what anyone else might be feeling.

Anna was right. Back then, if she had told me she was worried about her father, I wouldn't have understood what she meant. I would have laughed it off and tried to distract her with a taste of moonlight or a quest for the end of the rainbow.

"I'm sorry," I said.

Anna's pale blue eyes widened. They studied my face, then dropped to the iron band around my wrist. It was scratched up and dull, and I wondered how well she could see it. One of the best things about the Realms, she'd told me once, was how bright and sharp the colors were; the bright contrast between colors made it easier for her to tell where one item ended and the other began.

"Don't be sorry," she said. "I'm glad to have spent time in the Realms. I loved it there. I loved it so much that I..." She bit her lip. Then she continued, and I could tell she had changed her mind about what she was going to say. "In the few months since I've been back, I've missed it every second. Even if it wasn't right of you to take me there, I'm glad you did. It was the best thing that ever happened to me."

I could feel my smile stretching the skin of my cheeks. "Me too."

Anna smiled back at me, then looked again at the iron band. I held my breath.

"You're different now," she said.

"I am," I said earnestly. "Completely different. Much more trustworthy."

Anna laughed. It lit up her face, and a memory flashed through me: her face creased with delight while a rainbow flowed around and over us, her hand gripping mine as we looked up in wonder. (We *had* found the end of the rainbow eventually.)

Oh, Clare, she had said. *This is the most beautiful thing I've ever seen.*

I wanted her to look at me like that again. Like I was someone who showed her wonderful things.

Someone she wasn't afraid of.

"Leave the band on," I said.

Anna squinted at me. "You're sure?"

I wasn't. I was already regretting it; the iron felt like hot sandpaper rubbing against my skin. But I nodded. "Yes. That way you won't have to wonder. When you're ready to believe that I'm on your side, take it off then."

"All right," Anna said slowly.

I waited, hoping that my offer would be enough to prove my good faith; that she would take out the key and slide it into the lock. I could almost feel the heavy wrongness of the band dropping off me, almost catch my breath in relief.

"Well then," Anna said, turning away from me. "Let's keep going."

———◆———

We didn't talk again until the clouds shifted to gray and pink, the sunset cutting a sharp line across the western sky. By then it was obvious that we were not going to reach the mountain before nightfall.

A turn in the path revealed a few tall brown trees ahead, and a low mass of green. A few minutes later we were in the mossy, dappled shadows of a forest. The trail continued through the woods, beneath brown branches crowded with dark green foliage and dotted with red and yellow leaves. The sudden dimness made it impossible to ignore just how close to nighttime it was.

"We should set up camp," I said.

Anna stopped walking. The dimness that strained my eyes must have looked like near darkness to her. "How?"

"Um." I had no idea. In the Realms, when Tom and I traveled far from court, there was always a convenient abandoned cottage or enchanted cloud castle around when you needed one. But the ground of this forest was covered with broken branches, dry brown leaves, and clusters of thick white mushrooms. There was nothing level enough to sleep on.

"We'll have to sleep on the path at the edge of the woods," Anna said. Her tone was vaguely familiar, and it took me a moment to recognize it: she sounded like I had when I was lecturing her about how to survive in the Realms. *Don't make noise in the Dark Woods, or you'll wake the dryads. You can't eat those cupcakes, they'll turn you to stone.*

I had thought I was being kind. Maybe Anna thought so, too, and couldn't hear her own condescension.

"I don't like the color of that sky, though," Anna went on. "We'll be in bad shape if it rains." A thin, high call rang through the air, and she tilted her head back to squint at the sky. "Is that a bird?"

I glanced up. Through the gaps in the foliage, a vast black bird, wings outstretched, soared in slow circles against the gray-white sky. There was something intent and focused about its flight, something fierce, even though its only movement was an occasional slight slant of its body—the air currents were doing all the work.

"Yes," I said.

Anna frowned. "That's the third time I've heard it since we left town. Can you make out what kind of bird it is?"

The bird tilted as it traced a slow arc across the sky.

"Looks like an ordinary hawk," I said with a shrug, and dropped my backpack onto the ground.

See? The fae can lie as well as anyone.

5

The attack came in the middle of the night.

I slept through the beginning of it.

To be fair, it had taken me hours to fall asleep. The small rocks that littered the ground lodged themselves in my lower back, shoulder blades, spine, and neck. Basically, anywhere my body jutted out the tiniest bit, there was a sharp edge to meet it. A cool wind had started to blow, carrying with it the scent of rain. It made the branches rustle and the leaves whisper, and I kept imagining I felt the first raindrops hitting my face. The iron band was an itchy weight around my wrist, sending pulses of discomfort up my arm.

Anna, maddeningly, had fallen asleep immediately, and she snored loudly and rhythmically. Which didn't make it any easier for *me* to fall asleep.

Her voice played over and over in my head: *I didn't know if you were ever going to let me out.*

All that time, I had thought we were friends, while she had thought I was holding her prisoner. And she didn't even know the real reason Tom had brought her to me.

I remembered it like it had been yesterday. It *had* practically been yesterday, by fae standards; several months ago, not long after the queen had started sending Tom out on expeditions into the human world. The expeditions were either a great honor or a terrible punishment—we had never been sure which—and I had hated them. They meant I was frequently alone for days or weeks, and every time Tom came back, he was different. I couldn't explain exactly how he was different, but I felt like I was losing him.

Then, after one of his quests, he brought me a playmate. I knew then that he understood how I felt and, more importantly, that he still cared.

I didn't question Anna's presence in the Realms or wonder about the life she had been taken from. The humans who found their way into the Realms were always so delighted to be there, at least in the beginning, and Anna was no exception. On her first day I took her to the lagoon to sit on the rocks watching for mermaids, and a baby mermaid had come over and combed our hair with a fork. Anna had clutched my hand and laughed, her face filled with delight.

When I finally fell asleep, I dreamed that Anna and I were dancing in a field of bright red poppies, violet-scented raindrops falling on our faces. That part was an actual memory; but in the dream, Tom was there, too, his lean face alight with joy, his hose and cloak a clash of purple and green. He held out his hand to me, and I pulled Anna with me as I ran to him.

"You're back!" I said, dancing in a small circle around him. "You're back, you're back!"

In reality, Tom was always grim when he returned from the human world, his face drawn and his lips pressed shut. But in the dream he laughed down at me, the corners of his eyes crinkling in delight.

"I brought you something," he said. "A magic mirror! Want to ask it questions?"

Then a shadow fell over us, and we turned.

"*Clare!*" Anna screamed. "Wake up! Help!"

I sat up in darkness, blinking, rocks shifting and rolling under me. My eyelashes had crusted over while I slept, and I had to peel one of my eyelids up. The moon was a smudged white circle surrounded by clouds, leaving the path shrouded in darkness. I heard grunts and squeals and screams, but I couldn't see anything.

Something large and furry scurried over my legs, and a pair of teeth sank into my skin just below one knee.

I rolled over and slammed my knee down, pressing the creature against some of the sharp-edged rocks. It squealed and let go of my leg, claws scuttling on pebbles as it raced into the woods. I sprang to my feet, clenching my fists and summoning knives to my hands.

It was instinct; I wasn't thinking about the fact that my magic was depleted and had been for weeks. To my surprise, though, the magic was there, filling the space around me. It surged within me like a breath of cool, fresh air after a month trapped in haze.

But the knives didn't come. The iron band went hot and heavy, and agony shot up my wrist and arm. I gasped in pain and let the magic go.

Something snarled at me from the shadows. A dark, furry shape, teeth flashing. I snarled back before realizing it wasn't alone. There were dozens of them forming a semicircle around me.

Rats.

I looked for Anna. Another dozen or so rats surrounded a tree, lunging and trying to scamper up its trunk. They were slightly larger than normal rats, but they still couldn't reach the lowest branches. One of them leapt and clung to a branch, nearly upside down. A booted foot emerged from the leaves and kicked the rat in its snout. It fell, squealing, into the cluster of snarling rats below.

Anna: located.

One of the rats in the semicircle around me lunged, and I tried Anna's trick, pivoting and kicking sideways. My aim wasn't as good as hers, and I only grazed the rat with the side of my boot. That was enough to make it fall back, but it immediately crept forward again.

A weight fell onto the back of my neck, and claws dug into the top of my spine. That was when I realized it wasn't a semicircle of rats. It was a *circle*. They were behind me, too.

I grabbed the rat by the scruff of its neck and flung it away from me. I reached for my magic again, and the band on my arm rewarded me with a surge of burning pain. But a hiss rose from the rats, and several of them cringed. They felt what I was doing. They were afraid of magic, and they didn't know I couldn't use it to attack them.

Or could I?

"Anna!" I shouted. "Throw me the key!"

The rats around the tree turned to look at me. Dozens of red eyes gleamed in the dark.

Anna's voice, shrill and shaking, came from the leaves. "I can't!"

"Are you *joking*? I'll put the band back on afterward, I promise!"

"No, I mean I *can't* throw it! I can't see you at all."

Good point. The last thing we needed was for one of the rats to swallow the key.

"I'll come to you!" I said, and drew on my magic again. The pain made me gasp, but the rats drew back. I took a step toward the tree where Anna was hidden.

The rats attacked.

They came in a surge, all of them at once. I had no time to react before they were upon me, a hissing, squealing mass of warm, heavy fur and prickly claws. I went down under their weight, and my head hit something hard.

Tom, I thought. *Tom, help me!* But there was fur in my mouth and I couldn't breathe, much less call for him.

I reached for magic again. The iron band turned to fire on my skin, but my terror was greater than my pain, and I kept pulling in magic while the rats scrabbled over me, even as the skin was scorched off my wrist.

This time, though, the rats didn't fall back. They had realized I couldn't use the magic. Teeth grazed my neck, and I yanked my arm up and struck the rat. I heard a sizzle as the burning band hit fur. The rat shrieked in pain.

Then I realized: I *did* have a weapon. The band turned hot when it canceled my magic, hot enough to burn.

I swept my arm in front of me, pulling in magic with all my might. Agony raced up my arm, and the smell of scorched fur filled the air. The rats squealed and hissed, and for a moment the space around me was clear.

I scrambled to my feet. My arm felt like it had burned down to the bone, and I couldn't stand the pain anymore. I let the magic go and stood gasping, glaring at the rats that were still only yards away.

One of them gathered itself and sprang at me, and I couldn't force myself to call fire into the band. I kicked instead, snapping my leg out the way Tom had taught me. This time, my foot hit the rat squarely in the snout, and it flew backward and hit a tree.

A snarl rose from the others, a cacophony of rage. At the same time, a rumble shook the sky, softly menacing: the sound of thunder, distant but getting closer.

I glanced at the tree where Anna was still hidden by foliage. It was too far away. I would never get there before the rats overwhelmed me.

This was a forest, though. There were trees everywhere. There was one just a few feet behind me.

I whirled and ran for it.

I realized my mistake immediately. It was a tall, bare tree with no convenient low branches to grab. I threw myself at it anyhow, scrabbling and digging my fingernails into the bark. But desperation and willpower were not enough. I fell back to the ground just as the rats behind me growled in unison.

I turned to face them, my back to the tree. My wrist throbbed, and I steeled myself to set it aflame again. Lightning flashed white through the sky, briefly illuminating the mass of rats, their beady eyes and yellow teeth. I didn't think the threat of magic was going to stop them, not this time.

They advanced, grim and steady, and I drew in my breath.

Then the skies opened and the rain came down in a torrent.

It was as if the clouds were buckets that had suddenly been overturned. The rain was sharp and icy, plastering my hair to my face and my clothes to my body. I blinked away raindrops, and in the moment before water poured over my face again, I saw the rats turn and run all at once, like one massive, undulating gray creature. They disappeared into the forest, their squeals fading.

The next roar of thunder was right on top of us, deep and loud and angry. When the lightning lit up the world again, it revealed nothing but me and the trees and the sudden small rivers flowing across the forest floor. And Anna, clambering down from her perch, feeling her way with feet and hands. She reached the ground and started toward me, then tripped on a root and fell with a splash into a puddle.

The rain felt cool and soothing on the iron band, turning it from fire to ice. It was almost enough to make up for my suddenly soaked clothes and dripping hair. I walked across the sodden ground to Anna, water squelching in my boots, and helped her up.

"My cane," she said. Her voice was hoarse from sobbing. "I left it . . ."

I thought of saying, *Give me the key first.* But it wouldn't work; Anna could get the cane herself if she really needed to.

I sloshed over to where we had been sleeping, making my way by feel and by the faint glow of the moon, its light diffused by the clouds. Our travel bags had been torn open—whatever food we hadn't eaten last night was destroyed—and the water bags were ripped and empty. The drawing of the two children was a sodden mass. A lump rose in my throat. I ignored it, got the cane, and handed it to Anna. I felt her fingers curl tightly around it, but she didn't move.

"I'm sorry," she said. "I would have tried to fight them off you, if I'd had something to hit them with. But I couldn't find my cane when I woke, and I didn't know where . . . I didn't . . ." Her voice trailed off. When she spoke again, it was in a whisper. "I was too afraid."

"It's all right," I said. "You couldn't have fought them all by yourself."

"But I could have given *you* something to fight with." She fumbled in her pocket and pulled out the tiny key. "Give me your arm."

I held my arm out, hardly daring to breathe. Anna's fingers were deft as she felt around the band for the lock, then slid the key neatly inside it. I forced myself to hold still as impatience thrummed through me and rain dripped down the front of my shirt.

The band fell from my wrist with a tiny click. It landed in the puddle spreading across the ferns at my feet.

An angry red burn circled my wrist, dotted with small, bumpy blisters. The rain hit it, cold and cool, and I let out a blissful breath.

Anna reached out and touched my fingers. "You're bleeding," she said.

"Oh." I rubbed the blood off on my soaked shirt. "I must have touched my leg. One of the rats bit me there."

Anna leaned over, touched the wound on my calf, then quickly drew her fingers away. The rain was letting up—it was still steady, but not the downpour it had been—and it ran in thin rivulets over her hair. "We had better clean that."

"Why?" I said. "I'll just keep it covered until it goes away."

"It might not just go away. It could get infected or ..."

She took in my confused silence. "In the Faerie Realms, do wounds always just go away?"

"Eventually," I said. "I mean, unless they kill you."

"Right. Well, here we have to be more careful."

I shrugged. "Now that the band is off, my magic will take care of it."

"That's good." Anna bit her lower lip. "You didn't scream."

"What?"

"You were so silent I thought . . . I was afraid you had died. Or that you had run away and left me." She blinked rapidly. "How could you not scream when you got that bite?"

"You should never scream when you're attacked," I said. "It just encourages whoever's attacking you."

Tom had told me that many times. Everyone in the Realms knew it. But it made Anna look at me in a way I didn't understand.

"We should get going," I said. Water dripped from my hair into my shirt, a constant clammy trickle running down my spine. "If we stay here, the rats might come back."

Anna wrapped her arms around herself. "I heard them go deeper into the woods. I don't think we should follow them."

"No," I agreed. "We'll go around the woods. I think

we can walk through the cornfields. It will take longer, but it will be safer, and we can stay in the fields until we're closer to the mountain."

The moon had emerged from behind the clouds, giving enough light for me to see Anna's frown. "We'll have to go through part of the woods eventually," she said.

"Yes, but only for a bit. And it will be full daylight by then."

Anna nodded and turned, leaning on her cane as if she needed it for her legs rather than her eyes. I wasn't sure why she was moving so slowly, but I was too wet and tired to care. I wrung out my hair—a stupendously futile gesture—and started toward the edge of the trees. Then I glanced back to make sure Anna was following.

And saw why she had been deliberately lagging behind.

She was leaning over the puddle, one hand in the murky water. She pulled out the iron band and dropped it swiftly into her pocket.

When she made her way toward me, she tried to do it swiftly. But in the dimness of the forest, she must have been close to truly blind. She stumbled several times on the rough ground, despite her cane, and had to slow down.

Which meant she couldn't see me watching her. I waited until she was right beside me, then turned my back on her and headed through the trees.

Neither of us said a word as we trudged, squelching and dripping, down the road in the direction we had come from.

6

I had been right about the breaks in the cornstalks;
they *were* paths, and they led between the cornfields.
By the time we reached the first of them, the sun had
risen high enough to warm my clothes and hair, if not
to entirely dry them. Anna walked right past the break
in the corn without seeing it and only stopped when I
called her name.

"I think we can cut through here," I said. "Then we'll
turn toward the mountain. We should get there well
before sunset."

Anna nodded and backtracked, squinting at the
towering stalks. I stepped into the break to show her
where it was, and she followed, falling into step beside
me. The path was barely wide enough for both of us, so
I kept my arms tight at my sides. Around us, the cornstalks rustled in the breeze.

After only a few steps, I had no idea which way we

were facing. The yellow and green stalks towered over us, and there was nothing in the empty blue sky that I could use as a landmark. It felt like I was in the Realms, where distance and direction mean nothing, and the longer you walk, the more likely it is that you are being tricked into going nowhere. It made me wish, more fiercely than usual, that Tom was with me.

I had to be careful about that. I was used to relying on my brother, and in his absence, I was going to want to rely on Anna, even though she had already tried to deceive me. I had to remember that until I found Tom, I was alone.

Something skittered among the cornstalks, and we both froze. A chipmunk, tiny and striped, dashed across the path in front of us and disappeared into the corn on the other side.

Anna let out a shaky laugh. "It's like when the town was infested. Any movement, any sound, made me think of rats." She shuddered. "But back then, it always *was* rats."

"And they were all that big?" I said. "Like the ones in the woods?"

"No. Some of them were huge, but most were the size of a normal rat." She made a face. "They weren't normal rats, though, were they? Not the ones that infected the town, and not the ones that attacked us in the woods."

"No," I agreed, and began walking again. "They weren't normal rats."

Anna hurried to catch up to me, her cane hitting the cornstalks in unsteady thwacks. "So what were they?"

"Fae."

"But they were so ugly," Anna objected. "I thought the fae were beautiful."

I had to switch my mindset back to human before what she was saying made sense. I struggled with how to explain it. "Fae can be beautiful, but not because it matters to them. They just like to be extreme. Extremely beautiful, extremely ugly, extremely grotesque . . . it's all the same. I'm not sure they even see the difference."

Anna was silent for a moment. Then she said, "I guess you only showed me the beautiful parts."

"Yes," I admitted. "I wanted you to enjoy yourself."

She shot me a quick, sideways smile. "I did. It was the best month of my life. That's why—" She broke off and went back to frowning. "If the rats were fae, then how could they be on this side of the border? Doesn't that violate the Pact?"

"Some fae can come here in animal form, if they wish." The Pact, like most faerie bargains, was very complicated. I didn't understand all the clauses and exceptions—no one did, which was part of the point—but I knew it had accomplished its main goal: it kept the fae from meddling in human affairs. While they *could* cross the border as animals, they rarely did. To be trapped in one shape, unable to use magic, was torture to the fae.

It was the reason Tom was so valuable to the queen: he was human, so the Pact didn't apply to him. She could send him on missions into the human world any time she wanted.

"Once I get too fae for that," Tom had told me, just before he left the last time, "she'll want to send you. But don't worry. I won't let her make you into one of her tools."

He wouldn't be happy to discover that I had ventured into the human world—even though I had done it to find him. Now the whole court would know that I was capable of it. That would make it harder for Tom to protect me.

But I'd had no choice. He'd never been gone for so long before. I had missed him so much I couldn't stand it anymore, and I had been terrified that something had happened to him.

I hadn't imagined what I would find when I got here.

The sun climbed higher, drying our clothes. Last night's rain seemed to have cleared the clouds away; only a single large bird broke the stretch of endless blue, its wings spread wide as it floated aimlessly. By the time the cornfields ended, my stomach was squeezed tight with hunger and my throat was dry.

We stepped out into a long, bare field covered with brownish-yellow mulch. The path had curved more than I realized; I could see the woods a short walk away, trees clinging slantwise to the upward-sloping ground. Straight ahead of us, across the flat yellow-brown field, stood a covered wagon with horses hitched to it.

"Look!" I said. "Travelers!"

Anna squinted. "I see a brown smudge . . . is it a tent?" Then one of the horses jingled its harness, and she stepped back. "It's a wagon and a horse?"

"Two horses." As I spoke, two men emerged from behind the wagon and began to check the horses' hooves. "And two men. Maybe they'll have food and water."

Anna gave me an incredulous look, as if she had not until this moment realized how naive I was. "If they do, they're hardly likely to share it with us."

I gave her the same look back. "I wasn't planning to *ask* them."

Her hand twitched toward the pocket where she had hidden the iron band. She crossed her arms over her chest. "You want to steal their food?"

"Take it," I said. "Not steal it."

"What's the difference?"

"It would only be stealing if they didn't see me do it."

Anna opened her mouth, closed it, then opened it again. "That's not how we look at it here."

"Huh," I said, like that was a complete surprise. (To be perfectly honest: that's not how we look at it in the Realms, either. But I was *really* hungry.)

"We should steer clear of them," Anna said. "We can just head into the woods."

I held a hand over my eyes to shield them from the sun. "Are they from Hamelin?"

"I have no idea," Anna said. "I can't make out their faces."

"One of them has red hair and a very thin nose. The other has no chin. It's like his face just slopes right into his neck."

"Oh," Anna said. "Yes. They're from Hamelin."

"Then they'll give us food," I said. "We'll tell them we're on our way to rescue their children." I strode across the field.

Anna grabbed my arm. She was surprisingly strong, and I stumbled. "Clare, no. They're dangerous."

"Why would they be dangerous?"

"*Most* people are dangerous! Just like most fae."

A few weeks ago, I might have believed Anna. But I had spent enough time in the human world by now to know the difference between the two. Humans had a tendency to care about each other. They could get over it pretty easily, but they needed a *reason* to get over it. Usually.

You never had to ask *why* one of the fae would hurt you. But you did need to ask when it came to humans, and Anna hadn't given me an answer.

Growing up, I had never been sure whether Tom and I were fae or human. There was no doubt that we had been born human, but living in the Realms had changed us. Tom more than me, because he spent more time at court and used magic more often—lately, he had even been able to generate his own magic, like a true fae—but neither Tom nor I were really human anymore.

I had asked Tom once whether it was because we had been raised by fae and learned to behave like them, or whether the magic seeping into us had actually changed our true nature. He had raised his eyebrows and said, *What's the difference?*

Which was one fae trait Tom had adopted pretty early. He liked being annoyingly mysterious.

I had no patience for that sort of thing. So when Anna said, "Just trust me," I snorted and turned my back on her.

"I'm hungry," I said. "Anyhow, there are two of them and two of us. What can they do to us?"

"We're children! They're full-grown men!"

I had actually forgotten that; in the Realms, neither age nor size tended to matter much. "We'll tell them we're going to find the children. They'll want to help us."

"I assure you, they won't. Come on, Clare. Let's just go to the woods."

Her voice slipped, and I heard her desperation. I turned around and stared at her. "Why don't you want me to talk to them?"

"I just don't."

Her face was white and pinched. I wavered. I was hungry, but once we were in the Realms, I could conjure up food. . . .

Her hand went into the pocket where she had put the iron band, as if she was touching it for reassurance. My stomach tightened.

"I'm going," I said. "You do what you want."

I strode across the field, moving as fast as I could. I could tell Anna was trying to come up with another reason to object.

Sure enough, as soon as she caught up with me, she said, "Wait. You can't—"

"Excuse me!" I yelled, as loudly as I could.

The two men jerked around and stared at us.

When we were within a few yards of the wagon, I stopped. "We are on a quest to get your children back,"

I proclaimed. "Can you spare some sustenance to help us until we reach them?"

Both men stared at me like I was speaking a foreign language, then looked at Anna as if she was a ghost who had risen straight from the ground. "What are you doing out here?" the chinless man demanded. "Get back—"

"I'm sorry," Anna interrupted him. "My friend didn't mean to bother you. We'll be on our way."

"On your way where?" The red-haired man's eyebrows—which, oddly, were not red but black—beetled together. "You shouldn't be here. You were supposed to come with us. Your father said—"

"What my father said," Anna interrupted him, "was not meant to be shouted across a field."

The man spat at the ground. "I wasn't shouting."

To be fair, he hadn't been. Then again, it wouldn't have mattered if he had; there was no one in hearing distance except the four of us. And the horses, who had gone back to grazing and didn't seem particularly interested. Clearly, *I* was the one who wasn't supposed to hear whatever he had been going to say.

One of the horses stamped a hoof and strained at its bit. Somewhere, a small animal rustled through the grass.

"All right," the chinless man said. He jerked his head

toward the wagon. "Get in. We're bringing them back to Hamelin anyhow."

"Bringing what back to Hamelin?" I asked.

"No," Anna said firmly. "Thank you for the offer, but we're going to get the rest of the children. Tell my father that things are going well, and the people have reason to hope. He'll probably want to make a speech about it."

"If things are going well," the red-haired man said, "why are you so hungry?"

"What," I interrupted, "is in the wagon?"

Anna gave me a hard look. "I'll tell you later."

"Will you?" I asked. "Because it doesn't seem like *telling me things* is high on your priority list."

"It's not important," Anna snapped. "And we need to get going!"

Before these men tell me something you don't want me to know? I smiled at her, feeling my mouth stretch a little too wide, the way one of the fae would smile. I hastily adjusted it to look more human. "I think we can spare a few minutes, since things are going *so* well." I stepped forward.

The two men moved as one, jumping to stand between me and the wagon. The redhead shifted, and I saw what he was holding in his hand: a large wooden club.

The chinless man drew a knife from his boot.

I let my smile widen again, giving them a hint of who

they were dealing with: not a defenseless human girl, but a creature raised among the fae.

The man with the knife blinked and hesitated. But the man with the club stepped forward, swinging his weapon low.

I smirked at him, and then the club hit me in the side as I reached for magic and came up empty.

I gasped in pain and doubled over. The man lifted the club again.

"The second blow," he warned, "will really hurt."

I couldn't speak. I could barely breathe. But worse than the pain was the humiliation. I had forgotten, again, that I didn't have magic here.

Fae have their own magic, but humans—even if they've been in the Realms for ages, like me and Tom—can only draw on others' magic. In the Realms there had been magic everywhere, and I'd taken whatever I needed. Sometimes I even took too much, and then Tom would have to drain some off me before I lost control of it.

Here, magic was harder to come by. Tom had told me about that, so I'd been prepared. I'd taken an object of power with me—a pair of magic glass slippers that Tom had given me—but after only a week, they were stolen by a human woman who needed them for a ball. After that, I'd had to learn to get by without.

But in the woods, I'd been able to draw on magic again. In retrospect, it was clear why. The magic I'd been pulling in had come from the rats, who were creatures of the Realms.

Here, I had nothing to reach for. And no way to defend myself.

Tom, I thought, the way I always did when I was scared. But he wasn't here either.

"Have it your way," the man said, and lifted the club.

Behind him, the horses suddenly snorted and reared, and the wagon creaked ominously. Both men whirled, just in time to see a huge, predatory bird swooping low over the field, headed toward us. One horse tried to bolt, and the other kicked at the rope attaching its harness to the wagon.

The man with the club dropped it to grab the reins. The chinless man ran to the other side of the wagon.

"There, now," he said, his voice low and soothing as he tried to calm the horses. "It's all right."

Above us, the bird shrieked. The horses were in full panic, straining to run, and the wagon lurched forward. One of the men swore, and I heard real fear in his voice.

"Let's go!" Anna hissed. "Quick!"

We turned and ran.

7

We didn't slow down until we reached the forest, its shade a relief from the sun beating down on us. Then, finally, I slumped against a large tree, breathing heavily. Anna sat on the ground, leaning back on her hands.

"What was *that* about?" I said, when I could speak again.

Anna snorted. "I think that was proof you should have listened to me in the first place."

"That's not what I meant! What were those men talking about?"

"I haven't the faintest idea." Anna got to her feet. "Did you get a good look at that bird? It seemed like it was diving at the horses specifically to scare them. Is that possible?"

"I haven't the faintest idea," I said coldly.

We looked at each other. Anna's face was shiny with sweat. I crossed my arms over my chest.

"Fine," she snapped. "Let's just keep going, then."

"That's an excellent plan." I turned and stormed up the path. My side ached ferociously where the club had hit me, but I forced myself to walk as fast as possible.

We trudged in silence for about ten minutes, twigs cracking loudly beneath our feet. Then Anna said, tentatively, "It's not that I don't want to tell you. It's more that I can't."

"What's stopping you? Your father?"

"Sort of. I made a promise . . ." She stumbled over a rock, and I reached out instinctively to help her. She shook my hand off angrily. "I can't talk about it. I *won't* talk about it."

Do the unexpected, Tom's voice whispered in my mind. *Keep them off balance.*

"All right," I said.

"And I don't have to—" She stopped, registering what I had said. "What?"

If you can't beat them, confuse them. It's almost as satisfying.

"You don't have to tell me anything." I smiled at her sweetly before turning. "Let's keep going."

Tom was right. Anna's expression was quite satisfying.

The forest deepened, the trees growing taller, the

shadows darker. The pain in my side got worse as I walked, and I continued to ignore it. I kept a sharp eye out for rats. But the trail was empty, the only sounds the twittering of birds.

Then I saw a cluster of berries, orange red and just ripening, scattered across some brambly leaves. I stopped short. I was so hungry that I felt it in my head rather than my stomach, a dull pressure inside my skull. Maneuvering my fingers between the thorns, I plucked a berry and examined it for a moment before popping it onto my tongue. It was plump and juicy, so it helped with my thirst as well as my hunger.

I had stuffed about a dozen into my mouth when Anna grabbed my wrist and pulled my hand away. "What are you doing?"

Since the answer seemed obvious, I yanked my hand out of her grip, a movement which made the bruise on my side burst into fresh pain. My fingers were covered with yellowish juice, and a drop splattered on Anna. She jerked away. "Stop! Those could be poisonous."

"They're not," I said, and crammed another handful into my mouth. "They're a little tart, though—not fully ripe. They'll be better in a week. If we're still alive in a week, we should come back here."

"How do you know they're not poisonous?" Anna demanded.

"I've had them before."

"Poisonous berries and nonpoisonous berries can look almost identical! Even to people who can see them in detail. Don't you know that?"

I hadn't known that. It slowed me down, but I had already eaten at least three fistfuls of berries, and I felt fine. Well, my stomach was churning, but that was only because this was my first bite of food all day. And my lips and tongue were tingling, but that was only because the berries were so tart. . . .

Anna shook her head in disgust. "All those lectures Tom gave me about how dangerous the Realms are, and I shouldn't accept food from anyone, and I shouldn't follow any cries or accept any dance invitations or pick any flowers . . . did he forget to warn *you* that the human world has its dangers, too?"

"He didn't get a chance to," I snapped. "He doesn't know I'm here."

Anna's eyes widened, and I flashed back to how things had been when she was with me in the Realms. I would never have taken a step without Tom's permission back then.

"Won't he be angry," she said, "when he finds out?"

"I don't care," I said, with more bravado than I felt. "I'm angry at *him*."

Anna didn't look convinced.

"Anyhow," I said, "it doesn't seem like I've been poisoned. Do you want some berries?"

"No, thanks," Anna said. "If you're still alive by nightfall, I'll think about it."

"By nightfall we'll be in the Realms," I pointed out. "There will be dozens of things other than berries that could kill me there." I grabbed another handful. They didn't taste nearly as good as they had—they were *definitely* not ripe yet—but I chewed defiantly. "Your loss."

Anna sighed heavily and led the way up the trail. She moved slowly, sweeping her cane carefully in front of her and holding her other arm diagonally up in front of her face. The path was strewn with rocks, and branches hung low over the trail. I almost passed her before I remembered how much she hated that. I fell into place behind her instead, forcing myself to move slowly enough that I wouldn't pass her.

I was so tense that I didn't realize the prickles running through me weren't just nerves. But when we finally came around a curve in the trail and found ourselves facing a sheer wall of gray rock, the tingling hit me so hard I stopped walking.

Anna was around the bend before she realized. She squinted back at me. "What's the matter?"

I doubled over and grabbed my stomach. "Oh no. Maybe you were right about those berries."

Anna's mouth dropped open. She looked around frantically, as if hoping an antidote would be hanging from one of the tree branches.

"Just joking!" I laughed, and straightened.

She glared at me. One of her eyes wandered outward, the way it sometimes did when she focused too hard. "Not funny."

Anyone fae would have found it hilarious. I could almost hear Tom snickering. I glanced up at the bird still floating lazily in the sky above us.

"Not funny. *Mean*," Anna added. "I'm nervous enough without you pretending you're not feeling well."

"I wasn't pretending," I said, trying to be conciliatory. "But it wasn't the berries. It's the magic. Can't you feel it?"

I knew she couldn't, even before she shook her head. (So maybe I wasn't feeling *that* conciliatory. I was still pretty angry about the wagon.) She looked up, shading her eyes and squinting. The cliffside was nothing but stark gray stone, with a few wiry plants clinging to its cracks, so she could probably see it as well as I could. "The townspeople who followed the children said Tom led them right into the mountain."

"Yeah, makes sense. That's one of the typical ways humans enter the Realms." It was how I had stumbled in, once upon a time: I had run right into a hillside, too young to know better. Tom had seen the rocks swallow me up and run in after me.

"So how do we get into the mountain?" Anna said. "Do we just start pressing on the rock until we find the spots where our hands go through?"

"No need," I said. "I can sense where the portal is."

Something rustled in the undergrowth. Anna jumped. "Why don't you do that, then?" she said tersely.

I turned, faced the gray cliffside, and put one palm flat on the side of the rock.

"This is the place," I said confidently. "Are you ready?"

"Yes," Anna said, leaning forward.

There was something odd in her tone, but I didn't have time to work out what it was. Soon I would be back in the Realms, and Tom and I would be together again. I closed my eyes, concentrated, and pushed my hand through.

A thorn bit into the base of my thumb. I pulled back. "Ouch!"

"What's the matter?" Anna said.

I pulled a thin green bramble out of my skin, dropped it to the ground, and put my hand on the rock again. I could feel the magic in the stone, shimmering against my skin. I pushed.

This time I wasn't near any thorns. But I pushed my hand so hard against the rough rock that I hurt myself anyhow, both my palm and the injury in my side pro-testing. I closed my eyes, ignored the pain, and put all my strength into my arm.

I already knew it wasn't going to work, though. I shouldn't need strength.

"Clare?" Anna said.

"Be *quiet*! I'm concentrating." The rock was hard and unyielding against my hand, and it shouldn't have been. It should have parted for me like a curtain, letting me step straight through into the magic that was so close it made my blood dance. Something was terribly wrong.

The queen had been known to bar her subjects from the Realms. It was the most terrible punishment she could inflict. But surely she wouldn't do that to *me*.

"Clare!" Anna cried, and I opened my eyes. Anna had her head tilted up, her eyes going in opposite direc-tions as she tried to focus on the sky.

The bird that had been circling overhead tilted in the wind and plummeted toward us.

It was even larger than it had looked—or maybe it grew larger as it dove. Anna screamed and cowered, and I found myself unable to move. The bird came at us, claws extended, hooked beak open, so close I could see the white and brown patterns on the undersides of its wings.

Tom, help. I managed to keep myself from screaming

it. Anna stumbled backward, away from the mountain, which was the wrong way to go. But I backed up with her.

The bird landed right in front of us in a whoosh of wind and feathers. As it landed it changed, lengthening and shifting into a tall, winged woman of astounding beauty, white skin and slashing cheekbones and narrow, soaring wings. Only the cruel yellow eyes and the gleaming black feathers were unchanged.

Beside me, Anna made a tiny whimpering noise, and the faerie's mouth curved upward. I held myself as straight as I could.

"Hello, Mother," I said.

Behind me, Anna sucked in her breath and stepped back, twigs crackling beneath her feet. I wished there was a way to tell her to be still, but I didn't dare glance at her. It's not a good idea to take your attention off the queen of Faerie, even for a second. Depending on her mood, she could easily take it as an insult. Or an opportunity.

I was fairly adept at reading my mother's moods. But I had developed that skill in Faerie, when she was surrounded by imps and goblins and other creatures also reacting to her whims, when Tom was there to help me with hints and warnings. Here in this mundane forest where she didn't belong, with the harsh sunlight casting her face into stark relief and making her wings shimmer blindingly, I had no idea what she was about to do.

So I watched her and waited, and hoped Anna would have the sense to do the same.

My mother smiled, and I forced myself to keep breathing, slowly and evenly. She folded her wings and tucked them behind her into an elegant curve as thin as a knife's blade. She was standing very close to the cliffside. In her true shape, she couldn't step away from the portal; like the rest of the fae, she could only enter the human world in animal form.

"My dear daughter," she said. "I have missed you. Where have you been?"

"Out playing with humans," I said, in the same careless tone. I turned slightly as I did, so my back was to Anna and I didn't have to see her expression. It was imperative that I not care about her reactions. "Have I been away long?"

"I'm not sure," my mother said. "I didn't notice that you were gone until I started looking for your brother."

She didn't say it to be cruel, and I didn't flinch. I had only a second to decide how to react, and nothing to base that decision on except her tone of voice. Did she know what Tom had done? Was she amused or angry? Was she truly looking for him, and if so, why?

I had been the adopted daughter of the faerie queen since I was a toddler, yet I could no more have answered those questions than on the day I'd first met her.

"Oh, good," I said, after hesitating a bit too long. "I'm looking for him, too."

"Are you?" The queen's smile stretched all the way around the sides of her face—a good sign; that was her amused smile. But with Anna behind me, I was aware for the first time of how grotesque it looked. "I don't think your chances are very good."

Was that a threat? A prediction? Either way, there was only one response I could think of. "I'll find him."

She shook her head. "You're so helpless out here. Not at all like your brother. I'm impressed that you've survived this long." She snapped her wings out. The edge of her right wing hit an overhanging branch and sheered it off; it fell to the forest floor in a crash of twigs and leaves. "If you come across Tom, tell him to come home. I am annoyed with him. He has something that belongs to me."

"I'll tell him," I said. "As soon as I find him."

"Are you having a hard time getting into the Realms?" She lifted an eyebrow. "I'm not surprised. You look more human than you did last time I saw you."

That was definitely a threat—or at least, it was if she remembered the last time she saw me, which had been at a ball where a faerie had offended her and she had turned him into a tree.

While I was still trying to decide how to react, the queen turned her back on me and put one long-fingered hand on the mountainside. The webbing between her fingers glimmered with rainbow colors, and the side of the mountain shimmered and vanished.

Anna caught her breath. There was now a dark, uneven arc in the side of the mountain, a doorway leading into blackness.

"He's in there somewhere," the queen said, twisting her head to look at me. She twisted it farther than a human could have, and Anna made a startled sound. The queen blinked at her.

"You," she said. "I hope *you're* not trying to get back into the Realms. Not without paying the price."

Now, at last, Anna was completely silent. Too late. I stepped up to the doorway in the mountain, drawing the queen's eyes toward me and away from Anna.

"Thank you, Mother," I said.

A rush of wind swept through the trees, followed by a soft, drifting cascade of yellow leaves. My mother looked me up and down and pursed her lips. "That's rather unsuitable," she murmured, and flicked a finger at me, keeping her other hand stretched into the portal.

A brief tingle ran up my skin. Instead of my itchy and smelly dress, I found myself draped in a light, gauzy lavender dress with a hem that fluttered right beneath my knees. Instead of the leather boots I'd picked up in a random town, I had delicate silk slippers on my feet. And the pain in my side was gone—probably because the bruise, beneath my clothes, had looked unsightly to my mother.

"Much better. You look lovely." My mother smiled, this time without showing her teeth. "Find him as fast as you can, Clare."

She flapped her wings once and rose into the air, so fast you couldn't tell if the blur was from her movement or her shape-shifting. A vast black bird caught an updraft, circled once overhead, then winged its way over the mountain and out of sight.

———◆———

It was a few seconds before the birds started chirping again. An animal rustled through the underbrush; a twig cracked. I took a step forward, toward the opening my mother had created in the side of the mountain. The ground was rough and rocky through the thin soles of my slippers.

"Wait." Anna grabbed my shoulder. "What just happened?"

"We can't wait," I said. "I don't know how long this passage will remain open."

My next step brought my slipper down on a tiny sharp rock, which sent a spasm of pain through my foot. I ignored it, stepping forward again. Then, abruptly, I was inside the mountain, cut off from sunlight, surrounded by dark and cold and damp.

There, hidden by the darkness, I let the tears trickle down my cheeks. I wasn't sure if I was crying because I was afraid, or because I missed Tom so much, or out of habit. When the queen turned her attention on me, I generally ended up in tears.

"Wait!" Anna said again, but her voice was right behind me this time. She had followed me in.

I had been hoping that she wouldn't—that she would be scared off—but the fact that she was here made my heart feel a bit lighter. I wiped my face with my sleeve, pulled in the magic all around me, and called up a circle of light. It hovered in the air above my palm, white and pulsating. By its glow, I could see a craggy, uneven tunnel with ridges and cracks all along its walls and stalactites hanging from its ceiling.

I closed my eyes, and my heart leapt. Here in the Realms, I could feel my bond with Tom again—and through it I felt his presence, faint and indistinct but unmistakable. He was in these caves. Not nearby, but close enough that we would be together again soon.

"Clare?" Anna said. "Was that—"

"Let's go," I said, and strode forward.

Right onto another sharp rock. I yelped, then set

my jaw and used the magic to turn my slippers back into boots. Cleaner, less mud-encrusted boots than I had been wearing before, though still not footwear my mother would approve of.

Anna followed me slowly, and I realized that to her, it was completely dark. I poured more power into the glow light until the cavern around us was bright as day.

"Thank you," Anna breathed. She reached out and ran a finger along one of my lavender sleeves. "Can you do something about my dress, too?"

"I suppose," I said. "But you won't find faerie clothes very practical once you're back. I learned that the hard way. They're not exactly made to last."

"I'll take my chances."

"You'll also," I said pointedly, "lose everything in your pockets."

She blinked. Her hand went to the pocket where the iron band was hidden, and then she snatched it quickly away.

"I guess you're right," she said. "It's not a good idea. Maybe after we find Tom."

"Why would that—" I broke off, suddenly understanding.

After all, when the mayor had prepared that iron band, he hadn't expected me to come marching into town. He hadn't known about me at all. That band had never been meant to trap *me*.

It had been meant to trap Tom.

The mayor must have been hoping Tom would come back. A futile, desperate hope . . . but in the end, someone *had* come. Me. And he'd seen an opportunity.

Anna had no intention of letting me persuade my brother to return the children. She was here with a weapon to use against him. And I was leading her right to him.

She looked at me, her eyes softly innocent, and I took a deep breath. It didn't much matter. Tom would be more than a match for her. *She* was a fool if she thought an iron band would let her triumph over a fae prince. She would never get close enough to him to use it.

So I wasn't betraying Tom by leading Anna to him. Once I found my brother, Tom and I would figure this out together, and whatever Anna was planning wouldn't matter at all.

I reached for magic and summoned up two loaves of travel bread. They were lumpy and smelled a bit stale—I had never been very good at magicking food—but I was too hungry to care. So was Anna, judging by the speed with which her loaf disappeared.

Once the loaves were gone, I summoned up

waterskins—the water was slightly salty, but not too bad—and then Anna and I stood looking at each other. Her expression had shifted slightly, into wary respect, and I hated how good it made me feel. She had seen me use magic plenty of times, after all. It hadn't made her like or trust me.

I turned abruptly away from her, making the waterskins vanish with a wave of my hand.

"Follow me," I said, and led her into the Realms.

9

"So," Anna said, a few minutes later. "That was your . . . mother?"

I remained a couple of feet ahead of her. It was a bit mean of me—the path was mud and clay littered with rocks, and despite the bright glow light, I knew she couldn't go as fast as I could. During the month we'd spent together, she had always been hesitant in unfamiliar places. But it was easy not to care about that in the wake of the faerie queen's presence. Her *not caring* was like a pervasive aura, spilling over me and reminding me how little anyone I knew would care about human feelings.

"Yes," I said. "The faerie queen adopted me and Tom when we stumbled into the Realms. Without her protection, we wouldn't have survived a day."

I wasn't sure why I felt the need to defend my mother

to Anna, but I was bristling all over, like a porcupine about to release its quills.

And the truth was, Tom and I were incredibly lucky that the queen's hunting party had come upon us that day, and that the queen had been in the mood to adopt small creatures. By the time her mood had worn off, most of the fae had accepted us as the queen's changeling children. Nobody could be sure how she would react if we were killed. By then, Tom was old enough to protect me, and he made sure we attracted the queen's attention from time to time, just to make sure that uncertainty continued.

"So, earlier, with the wagon . . . that was also her? Protecting you?"

"Looks that way." I didn't feel like getting into the whole truth: that if my mother had been protecting me, it wasn't because she cared about *me*. It was because she wanted me alive for some reason of her own.

And now I knew what the reason was. She was using me to find Tom.

"I never knew my mother," Anna said wistfully. "She died when I was only a baby. My father did his duty, he kept me clothed and fed, and taught me as best he could, but . . ."

She trailed off. I suspected I was supposed to say something, but I was too busy examining our surroundings.

The walls were a mass of swirling rock formations, brown and gray and white, and many-veined stalactites pointed down at us from the ceiling. To our left, a bunch of stalactites had joined together, and they rippled over the walls like an eternally still waterfall. To our right, stones shaped like giant wings bulged out at us.

Even without the feel of magic all around me, and without the tinge of Tom's presence through our bond, this unearthly, disturbing beauty would have told me we were in the Realms.

"... but," Anna finished, when it became clear I wasn't going to speak, "I'm never really sure whether he loves me. I think he tries, but if he truly did love me, he wouldn't have to try so hard."

Oh. *Oh.* She was trying to draw a connection between us. But she was getting it all wrong.

I thought about explaining that the faerie queen didn't love *anyone*, so I didn't have to live with that kind of uncertainty. But I doubted Anna would understand.

Anyhow, she was still talking. "He's always locking me into my room for one reason or another. He says it's because he's worried about me getting hurt. But it seems like anything that's even the tiniest bit fun could get me hurt."

The faerie queen had locked me up once, in a tiny, dark cave filled with giant spiders. She hadn't bothered to pretend it was for any reason other than because she was angry. I no longer remembered what I had done to anger her. I only remembered crouching in the darkness, drawing desperately on magic to keep the spiders away, waiting for Tom to come rescue me. By the time he had, dashing beneath the spiders and slashing at their long, spindly legs with a stolen sword, I had pulled in so much magic that it had taken him half a day to draw it out of me.

He had only found me because of our bond, which he had forged so he could keep me safe. I had never before used it so that *I* could find *him*, and I couldn't tell if I was drawing closer. But there was only one way to go anyhow, so I kept walking.

"He doesn't trust me to take care of myself," Anna went on, "because of my poor eyesight. Or so he says. I think it's just an excuse."

She fell silent, clearly waiting for me to respond with a story of my own, to act like we had something in common. But we didn't.

Anna cleared her throat in the silence. "People say he used to be different. The townspeople tell me that after my mother died, something in him went hard. He always says it's just the two of us against the world, that we can't rely on anybody else or care about anybody else. That you do whatever you have to in order to make sure you don't get hurt."

I turned my head and blinked at her in surprise. Maybe we had been raised similarly after all. Except that in the Realms, nobody had to *say* that you should only care about yourself. It was so obvious that nobody would bother. It was the *two of us* part that was odd, that was unique to me and Tom.

"I believed him." Anna took a deep breath. "I never had a friend until you brought me to the Realms. That's why I . . . Clare, I have to tell you—"

A squeak sounded in the tunnel behind us. We froze. It sounded like a rat.

Without any need for discussion, we strode down the tunnel. Anna's cane tapped swiftly on the ground, then hit a rock outcropping, making her stop short. I reached for her hand. She resisted for a moment, then let me lead her.

The passageway got narrower and the ceiling lower. I ducked under a low-hanging rock, then called a warning to Anna. But she had already avoided it.

We kept walking until we reached a spot where the ceiling was covered with feathery crystals, pure white with tinges of rust and green. It felt like we were very, very deep inside the mountain. The tunnel still curved endlessly into darkness ahead of us, and the air was completely silent and still.

I kept a wary eye on the ridges and curves of the passageway and the shadows they created. But nothing moved, and I couldn't feel any magic.

Anna cleared her throat. "You thought it was a rat, too, right?"

"I did," I said. "But maybe we jumped to the wrong conclusion. There must be lots of small creatures and insects that live underground."

Judging by her expression, that didn't make Anna feel any better. "Well, I don't hear it now. But are we getting anywhere? It feels like we're walking in circles."

That was a good question, and one I paused to consider. My sense of Tom through our bond was still vague; no help there. I bent, picked up a sharp rock, and scraped it hard against an uneven ledge that jutted out from the side of the tunnel—once, twice, three times, making three parallel lines like the marks of an animal's claws.

Anna squinted. "Are you doing that to make sure we can find our way back?"

"No." It was a good idea, but it was too late to start now. Anna should have realized that; clearly she was just too scared to think straight.

I pulled in magic and made the lines bright white so she could see them more easily. I didn't even feel a strain—we were in the Realms now, with magic every-where. Which also meant that distance didn't mean much, and most paths *would* lead in circles.

So I was not at all surprised when, after another twenty minutes or so of walking and a couple of close calls with low-hanging rocks, I saw the three parallel lines on the wall to our right.

I pointed. Anna bent and skimmed her fingers along the rock until they reached the scratches. Then she let out a tiny whimper—so tiny I might not have heard it if not for the way the tunnel made every sound echo.

"We *are* walking in a circle," she said. "But . . . then why haven't we seen the opening we came in through?"

That seemed too obvious to require a response. Or maybe not, if you hadn't grown up in the Realms. Maybe in the human world, you generally *could* back-track if you'd gone the wrong way.

That must be nice.

I made the glow light even brighter, until Anna winced and shielded her eyes. Now I could see the passageway ahead curving into gray waves of stone, but there was nothing in it.

The fae liked setting traps, but they usually weren't curious about the results; they were happy to leave humans in them for years and years, not bothering to check on them until long after they had died of hunger and thirst. Some fae created marvelously ingenious booby traps and then forgot about them entirely. I had stumbled into more than one, and not once had the faerie who created the trap come to watch me die.

Nor had I ever gotten out of one by myself. It had always been Tom who saved me, who noticed I was missing and followed our bond and found me before it was too late.

"Clare?" Anna's voice was thin and pleading; she expected *me* to save *her*. To save us. "Are we trapped?"

That also seemed too obvious to require an answer. But I understood the real question she was asking.

"I can get us out," I said. (See? I'm *very* good at lying.) "But the children came through this way, and we're here to find them. There must be another gateway that leads deeper into the caves, to where Tom went. I just have to find it and open it."

Two things I had no idea how to do.

Anna's brow furrowed. Her lips parted as if she was about to say something.

Then, in the silence, we both heard it: the scrabble of claws on rock.

Anna's eyes widened. I turned around just in time to see a horde of rats race around the curve and pour through the passageway in our direction.

10

They came in a brown mass, spilling out of the darkness, a river of beady red eyes and snarling teeth. They covered the entire space between the tunnel walls, their squeals echoing among the rocks.

I called upon magic. It came in a rush, and the rats stopped as if they had hit a glass wall. They piled on top of each other, scrabbling and squeaking, hundreds of eyes glowing where my magic light touched them.

Anna gasped like someone who had just escaped drowning. "How long can you hold them off?"

I wasn't sure. There was so much magic here, enough for me to draw on forever. But humans weren't meant to hold this much; I could feel myself shaking already. Instinctively, I curled one hand into a fist and stuck my pinkie finger out, making the signal Tom had taught me, the one that meant *I need help*. Then I realized what

I was doing, forced my fingers apart, and flattened my hand against my legs.

Behind us, claws clicked on the rocks.

I whirled.

A single rat sat on the ground. It was huge—the size of a large dog—and its fur was so black it was hard to make out any of its features. Then it tilted its head, and the light glinted off its eyes.

"I call for truce," it said. "I am the prince of rats, and I would speak to you."

I sucked in my breath, and pitched my voice low so it—no, *he*—couldn't tell it was shaking. *Never let them see weakness.* "Do you know who I am?"

Anna blinked. "Clare? Are you talking to the *rat*?"

The rat hissed. "You are the sister of the prince who betrayed us."

"Then you know," I said, "that I am a princess of the Realms. If you harm me, you risk the wrath of the queen."

It's always best to establish your source of power up front.

"Do I?" the rat prince said. I knew how his voice sounded to Anna—all squeaks and gnashes—even as his meaning was clear to me. "Did you not leave your mother's kingdom without her permission? I am not sure she would grieve your death."

"She probably wouldn't," I agreed. "But she would still find it insulting."

"I may find that worth the risk," he snarled. "Your brother has gone too far. He doesn't care about much anymore, but I believe *your* death would still bother him."

"Clare," Anna hissed. "Do you *understand* those sounds?"

I was starting to feel dizzy. I couldn't tell if it was from the strain of holding the rats off or from fear. I made a quick decision. "Truce. Send your subjects away and we'll talk."

"I don't need to send them away," he said. "They will not attack you."

I knew that his statement was a challenge, or a test, or a trap—but I had been so long among humans that I couldn't immediately figure out which, or how best to respond. Tom would have said not to show fear, but which response was not showing fear?

"Send them away," I said again. "They're making my companion uncomfortable."

The rat prince laughed scornfully. But behind me, the rats turned and scrambled away. I heard their squealing and rustling fade and then vanish.

I let the magic go, and tried not to sag with relief.

The rat prince watched me, his eyes sharp, and I wondered if I had made a mistake. But all he did was rise on his back legs so that he was nearly as tall as a man. He coiled his tail against the ground, supporting himself on it, and bared his teeth at me. Arguably, it was meant to be a smile.

Anna tried to swallow a shriek. The result sounded like she was choking on her own breath.

The rat prince tilted his head. "What is wrong with the human girl?"

"I believe she finds your appearance alarming."

"Ah. Well, that's easily fixed." The rat prince shrugged, and in one quick ripple, he was no longer a rat. He looked like a boy, tall and square-jawed with a shock of blond hair. He wore leggings and soft boots and a purple cloak, and there was not a single thing about him to suggest rodent.

Which, to me, made him look more like a rat than before.

But Anna had not been brought up in the Realms. She let out a relieved breath, and when the young man bowed to her courteously, she smiled. It was an oddly shy smile, and it took me a moment to understand why: the light was bright enough, and he was close enough, that she could probably make out how handsome he was.

Humans are always deceived by appearances. Tom had said that so often I'd started teasing him about it.

"It is better that I wear this form," the rat prince said. His voice was low and smooth, and he spoke easily in the language of humans. "The other children, too, will find it less frightening."

"The other children?" Anna repeated. "Do you know where they are?"

"Not exactly. But they're somewhere inside the mountain, and I do know how to get out of this passageway." He lifted his eyebrows—which were, I noted, shaggier than human eyebrows tend to be. Every fae disguise has some small imperfection like that. "Would you like me to show you?"

"Oh! Yes, that would—"

I cut Anna off by stepping in front of her. "What," I said, "do *you* want with the children?"

"Nothing at all," the rat prince said. "I merely want to talk to your brother. But I can't find him, and I believe you can."

I was one hundred percent sure he was lying. But did it matter? I could sense the army of rats in the darkness, just out of sight. My feet ached from walking in circles around the passage.

"Just you," I said. "Leave the other rats behind."

"Of course." The rat prince shrugged. "My subjects

are not important in all this. They're merely a distraction."

I touched my calf where the rat had bitten me in the forest. My skin was completely healed, but I could still feel a cold, empty ache, like the echo of pain. "Oh, is that all."

"Well," the rat prince said modestly, "they're a very *good* distraction."

I pressed my lips together. "All right. How do we get into the rest of the caves?"

"We walk." He gestured toward the dark corridor behind us—the one I suspected was seething with rats. "I don't know how you missed it the first time."

I folded my arms across my chest. "Poor sense of direction, I suppose. This time, you can lead us."

"It would be my pleasure."

He was so smug. This was definitely a trap. The problem was, we were already in it, and I couldn't see any way out.

"Come along," the rat prince said, and walked past us. In the darkness, his subjects rustled and squeaked.

"This tunnel just goes around and around in a circle," I objected.

"Of course it does. You were never supposed to follow the tunnel." He glanced at Anna. His eyes were a pale, almost colorless blue, framed by silky golden lashes. "I apologize."

Before she could ask *For what?*, he was a giant rat again. Anna jumped and shrieked.

He winked at us—and let me tell you, seeing a rat *wink* is worse than just seeing a rat—then turned sideways and slid below a jutting rock.

"Follow me," he called.

I looked at Anna. She looked at me. We both knelt and peered beneath the overhanging rock, into the low, narrow, dark passageway beneath it.

"I don't know if this is a good idea," I said. (A rather vast understatement.)

"Do we have a choice?" Anna asked.

Which basically summed it up.

I pushed the glow light down and under the ledge, then got to my hands and knees and peered into the passageway, trying to figure out how far it went. In the faint glow ahead, I saw the rat prince's tail twitch. Behind me, Anna got to her hands and knees, her cane thudding against the rock.

I ducked my head under the ledge and squeezed into the passageway.

11

I took a deep breath, which was a mistake; my mouth immediately filled with dust. The glow light bobbed ahead of me, revealing craggy walls, brown and gray and white, dotted with feathery white moss. Ahead of me, the rat prince's claws clicked on the rocky ground. Behind me, Anna's breath was quick and shallow, her cane bumping against the rocks as she dragged it along.

This was *such* a mistake. In a narrow space like this one, the rat prince had all the advantages. I couldn't even try to imagine what Tom would tell me to do, because Tom would never have let me get into a situation like this.

The ceiling kept getting lower. Ahead of me, I could hear the rat prince's fur brushing the walls. Before long, I couldn't even crawl on my hands and knees. I had to lie on my stomach, breathing in dust and the very distinct, thoroughly unpleasant smell of rat fur. I dug into the dirt with my fingernails and pulled myself forward as fast as I could, dragging my legs behind me.

Then the light went out.

I bit down on my scream. The darkness was so total that there was no difference between the stone wall right next to me and the air in front of me. It was all just blackness.

I reached for more magic, but it wasn't there. I could feel the rat prince's magic, but he was powerful enough to hold it close, accessible to no one but himself.

"Sorry about that," the rat prince said. "These caves wind in and out between the Realms and the human world. We just hit a human spot, so your glow light won't work here. Once we're out of the tunnel, we'll cross back into the Realms."

"You could have warned us," I said through gritted teeth. My heart was pounding so hard it felt like it was taking up my entire chest.

The rat prince's tail slid along the rocks with a faint, dusty sound. "That wouldn't have been nearly as much fun."

I chose not to reply. Mostly because I couldn't think of anything to say.

"I didn't realize it would frighten you that much," he added. Not apologetically, but as if we had given him a delightful surprise. "It doesn't bother *me* at all. I can see in the dark. Not that I need to see. I prefer to feel my way along with my whiskers."

Something touched my feet, and I almost screamed again. But it was only Anna, who was suddenly moving a lot faster.

Which, actually, seemed like an excellent idea.

I pulled myself forward, my shoulders scraping the rocks, not stopping even when my head bumped against a low overhang. Finally the tunnel ended, and I stood up cautiously, dust raining down from my hair.

I was shaking, and it wasn't just from the total darkness and the small space. It was from that moment when the magic around me had failed, sharply and suddenly, leaving me completely at the mercy of one of the fae. Nothing but a small, frail human girl without anyone to protect her.

My panic didn't make any sense—I had been without magic for *weeks* now; I'd thought I was used to it—but I kept fixating on that sickening feeling when I had reached for it and it hadn't been there. I was *still* reaching for it, I realized, even though I knew it wasn't there. I couldn't make myself stop.

Anna scrambled out beside me. A light flickered on several yards away, revealing a small cave with uneven ledges jutting out from the curving walls. The rat prince sat on one of the ledges, back in his human form. He smiled at us, teeth flashing white, blond hair tousled. "Sorry about that. If it bothered you, we can try to avoid human spots from now on."

"I would appreciate that," I said coldly.

He got to his feet. "Rats are creatures of the Earth. I can feel where the ground is soaked with magic and where it is not." He walked toward a narrow opening in the rocks, his glow light bobbing at his shoulder. He stuck close to the walls of the cave, the way a rat would, instead of walking straight through it. "If you tell me which direction to head in, I'll show you the safest route."

Anna looked at me. In the dim light, her eyes were huge and dark, her terror almost palpable. The rat prince's glow light wasn't as bright as the ones I had made, and I doubted she could see anything. I tried to think of something reassuring to say.

"We still don't have a choice," was what I came up with.

She nodded and reached for my hand. I could feel her fingers shaking.

"How will *you* know which direction to head in?" she whispered.

"There's a bond between me and Tom. He bought

the spell from a sea witch, and he reinforces it every year at midwinter. I always know where he is, and he always knows where I am."

"Sounds useful," Anna said.

"It is." I swallowed. "Though I don't think Tom expected me to use it to lead anyone *else* to him."

Anna's hand tightened on mine. "I'm sorry," she said. "It wasn't supposed to . . . I didn't know it would be like this."

"Like what?" I squeezed back. "This is just a regular day in the Faerie Realms. We'll talk when something interesting happens."

She managed a little laugh, and together, we followed the rat prince.

Halfway across the dark cave, I stepped across an invisible border into the Realms. All at once, magic surrounded me, and it was like I could breathe deeply again after being trapped in too-thin air. Relief rushed through me, and I pulled the magic in.

It surged into my blood and bones, too swift and too vast, an overwhelming deluge. I felt as if my body had lit up from head to toe, my skin barely holding in the power.

The rat prince froze in midstep at the opening in the rocks. He turned his head to stare at me, craning his neck farther than was humanly possible, his eyes glinting in the dimness. His lips were pressed tightly together, but I was sure that if he opened them, his teeth would be long and sharp.

Anna looked from me to him uncertainly. I suspected she couldn't make out his expression and knew only that he had gone motionless. "What . . . ?"

"Be careful, Princess," the rat prince breathed. The magic hammered at my bones. I knew he could feel how close I was to losing control of it. Instinctively, I curled one hand into a fist, sticking my pinkie out. Then I made myself stop, because Tom wasn't there to help me, to take my hand and draw some of the magic from me. There was only the rat prince, and he remained perfectly still, coiled like the predator he was.

"What's going on?" Anna demanded. She was trembling so badly that her cane was shaking.

"I have too much magic." My voice quavered with the strain. "I've never tried to control this much. I should never have drawn it in."

"Well, it's too late for that," Anna said. There was a weird note in her voice, almost like she was . . . jealous? "So why don't you do something with the magic and get rid of it that way?"

I blinked. I had never *used* this much magic—it was

much safer to let Tom control it. Letting so much loose at once could have unpredictable side effects. But Tom wasn't here . . .

The rat prince drew his lips back. I looked up at the stalactites, then stretched out my fingers and let the magic go.

It streamed from me in a rainbow burst, a sparkle-filled cloud that lit up the cave and sent hundreds of colors swirling against the rocks. From within the clouds, new colors burst out of nothing, shifting and wavering. They wove in and out of the columns, danced with the shadows, narrowing and bursting over and over again.

Anna made a small, astonished sound and shielded her eyes. I tried to say something, but I had lost control of my body and my magic both. The sparkles spread, taking form, melting into each other, swirling into new colors. Now they ran over the walls like a rainbow, lines of light that went up and down and sideways, shifting and shimmering.

And finally, after an eternity of aching beauty, fading away.

But not entirely. When I blinked back into control of my body, gasping as if I had just run for miles, the cave was not the same. The rocks were no longer gray and white; they were streaked with soft reds and greens and violets. The ceiling sparkled with colorful constellations, as if we were standing beneath a distant, magical sky.

Anna stood with her head tilted back, her face dazzled. The rat prince watched me, his eyes still glittering and hungry. But when he spoke, his teeth were short and even—if a little too white to be believably human—and his voice was calm.

"Impressive," he said. "All this time, we thought you were nothing but Tom's main weakness. Maybe we were wrong."

I almost said thank you. Instead, I turned my back on him.

"Wow," Anna breathed. She stepped over to a stalagmite and put her face right next to it, circling it slowly and squinting. "It's beautiful."

It was—more beautiful than she knew. With the magic gone, I could see only what she saw—well, probably a more detailed version of what she saw: dozens of colors turning this small cave into a place of wonder. But unlike Anna, I knew there weren't dozens of colors. There were hundreds. A moment ago, I had seen them all; now they were hidden from my inadequate human eyes.

I glanced once more around the shimmering, multi-hued cave, filled with colors I could no longer see. I suddenly felt like I was going to cry. No wonder the human world always looked so dull and gray, when it was missing *this*.

How could Tom bear to spend so much time there? Once I found him, after I convinced him to return the children, we would figure out a new way for him to serve the queen. One that didn't force him into the human world and didn't constantly drive us apart. Maybe Anna could stay with us sometimes, and then it would be the three of us. . . .

"I forgot," Anna said, and her tone was a perfect match for how I felt. "I forgot how gorgeous everything is here."

The rat prince crossed to Anna, still sticking close to the walls instead of walking across the cave. He knelt next to her. She looked at him, surprised.

"It's not every human who can see the wonder in the Realms," he said softly. "Most see only the dangers and are frightened by them. There's something different about you."

I snorted.

The rat prince gave me a reproachful look. Anna didn't notice; she was too busy staring around the cave.

"I want to stay here," she said. Her voice shook. "I don't want to go back."

Which, despite the rat prince's compliment, made her just like every other human who wandered into the Realms. My half-formed fantasy vanished as I remembered what happened to all those other humans, the ones with no one to protect them.

"Really?" I said. "How did you feel about this place when we were being attacked by an army of rats?"

"The beauty is intertwined with danger," the rat prince agreed. He reached for Anna's hand, and she let him take it. "But don't worry. I'll make sure you don't get hurt."

"Excuse *me*," I snapped.

The rat prince glanced over his shoulder at me. He had changed his appearance subtly, making his cheekbones sharper and his shoulders broader. "I'll make sure nothing hurts you, either," he said with a noticeable lack of enthusiasm.

"That is *not* what I meant! How, exactly, can you make sure nothing hurts her?"

He turned back to Anna. "I'll do whatever it takes," he promised.

"Which doesn't answer my question."

He gnashed his teeth, then caught himself and smiled tightly. "Perhaps I'll do whatever Tomasakinolan did to protect you. Before he left you behind, that is."

I flinched before I could stop myself.

Anna shot the rat prince a sideways glance. Then she pulled her hand from his and crossed the cave to me. I summoned up my own glow light, not wanting to rely on the rat prince's.

"All right," Anna said. She lifted her chin. "Lead on, Clare."

The rat prince sighed, as if he admired her courage and respected her loyalty even though she had wounded him deeply. I had to admire the skill it took to get all that into one sound.

Anna's hand slid into mine. I didn't know whether I had reached for her or she had reached for me. I also couldn't tell which of us was squeezing more tightly.

We moved at the same time, our footsteps in sync, punctuated by the light, steady tapping of Anna's cane as we headed into yet another dark tunnel.

12

"Tomasakinolan?" Anna asked. "Is that really his name?"

We had been walking for some time now. Long enough for me to calm down and start breathing normally again. Long enough to get used to the constant scuffling in the shadows and the occasional gleam of beady eyes. Long enough to be sure that even though this craggy stone tunnel looked exactly the same as the one we'd been in earlier, we were no longer walking in circles. I could feel Tom's presence more clearly, getting steadily closer.

And long enough, apparently, for Anna to forget that the suave, handsome boy walking next to us was actually a fae prince who was only temporarily refraining from unleashing his army of giant rats on us.

"Yes," I said, before the rat prince could reply. "That's his full name. He goes by Tom, though."

He'd told me once that our mother, our human mother, had called him Tom. I had grown up believing it, until one day I'd realized it didn't make sense. The queen had renamed us both to her liking, and she wouldn't have cared what Tom was called in the human world.

"I can see why." Anna looked at me sideways. "Do *you* have a longer name, too?"

The rat prince looked scandalized. I sighed. "I do," I said. "But don't ask me for it. True names have power."

"Then why does . . ." She stopped, clearly realizing that the rat prince had never given us *his* name. "Why does, er, *he* know Tom's name?"

A good question. And one I didn't expect the rat prince to answer.

Sure enough, he just flashed us a smile and said, "You can call me Per."

Anna smiled back. I did not.

My actual name is Claranoradaka. Long, fancy names were a fad at the fae court for a while, started by a goblin king named Rumpelstiltskin. Because names have power, he thought that having a complicated, hard-to-remember name would make him safer. The fad lasted a very short while before Rumpelstiltskin's long, supposedly undiscoverable name was used against him by some human queen. After that, everyone started going by the first syllable of their names. (So that ended up *really* badly for Rumpelstiltskin, who wasn't happy about the first syllable he ended up stuck with.)

"I know his name," Per went on, "and he knows mine. We exchanged them when we agreed to work together."

Exchanging names was a fairly significant act among the fae; not quite as rare as Per was making it out to be, but still not something you did carelessly. If Tom had been willing to give his name in exchange for the rat prince's help, then this mission must be very important to him. He'd wanted to be sure he succeeded in stealing the town's children.

But why? Tom had failed to carry out the queen's commands before, without much consequence—most recently, when he traded a bag of magic beans and failed to get anything in return. Our mother was annoyed, but we knew how to deal with that. (Mostly by hiding until she got bored with being angry.) He'd never gone to such drastic lengths to bring her what she wanted.

"Why did you have to work together?" Anna asked the rat prince. "If Tom wanted the children and he had the pipe, why didn't he just go in and take them?"

There was a short, shocked silence.

"The fae don't just *take* things," I explained. "There always has to be an exchange of some sort."

"Because of the Pact?"

"No. Because that's how things work. Anything else would be"—I struggled to think of the right word—"rude."

"Rude?" Anna repeated incredulously. *"Rude?"*

That wasn't exactly it, but I couldn't think of a better word. "Imagine if being impolite made you so ashamed you wanted to die. It's kind of like that."

Per looked amused. I tried to ignore him.

Anna's brow furrowed. "But there were other humans in the Realms..."

"They agreed to come. Like you. Or they were lost and wandered in by mistake, like Tom and me. Or else were in love with one of the fae, which makes it totally different."

She blinked at me in confusion, and I sighed. "Fae etiquette rules are complicated."

"But don't worry," Per put in. "I'll be your guide among the fae. And I'm better at explaining things."

"Oh, really?" I turned to him with relief. "Explain this, then. If you and Tom are such good friends now, why do you need *me* to help you find him?"

"Who says I do?"

"Well," I said, "I did consider the possibility that you were helping us out of the goodness of your heart. Then I realized that I obviously haven't eaten for a while, because my mind is not functioning clearly."

Per looked at Anna. "She's not entirely wrong," he said. "I didn't even know I had a heart, until I met you."

I groaned. "*Stop*. You're not nearly as good at this as you think you are."

Per looked offended. "I am *very* good. In this form, I have lured dozens of girls to their doom."

A rock skittered beneath Anna's feet.

"Not you," Per assured her, giving her a distracted but soulful look. "For your sake, I will briefly suspend my murderous ways."

"Um ...," Anna said. "Thanks?"

"He hasn't lured anyone to their doom," I snapped. "He can't leave the Realms in his human form, and fae girls are more than a match for him. You're probably the first girl he's met in a hundred years who *isn't* a match for him."

Anna looked like she wasn't sure whether to be relieved, frightened, or insulted.

"That's not entirely true," Per murmured. "Let's not forget about you. Now that you don't have your brother protecting you, you're no more special than any of the human girls you hold in such low regard."

"Tom is still protecting me," I retorted. "And if you hurt me, you'll have to answer to him."

"Your brother has his own problems. He's no longer the queen's favorite, not now that he stole her children.

Rumor has it that he's in hiding. From me, from the queen, from all of us. Nobody can find him."

I stopped short, a sickening understanding rising from my stomach and filling my body. "Nobody except me."

Per brushed a stray lock of blond hair away from his face. "Rumor has it, he established some sort of bond with you. That's how he always saved you when you got yourself into trouble." He glanced over at Anna. "Which she did fairly often, by the way. Humans don't survive long in the Realms if they don't have a protector."

Anna looked from me to Per and back again. She was squinting ferociously, and I wondered how much of our expressions she could actually see. "Isn't Tom human, too?"

"He was," Per said. "But magic changes humans, and Tom uses so much of it. By the time he was your age, he was using it the way one of us would have. Tom is exceptional, for a human." He shook his head. "If he hadn't been saddled with his sister, he could have gone so far."

"If you're trying to get me to help you," I said, "you have an interesting way of going about it."

Per laughed. "Do you plan to abandon the children just to spite me?"

"I'll have to think about it," I ground out.

"I don't think you will." He lifted his eyebrows, which

had once again grown shaggy. "That is, if it's really the children you're after."

"What else would I be after?"

"Come now. Why are you really doing this? To save the children, or to save your brother?"

I knew I shouldn't let him get to me. But I couldn't help it. I had forgotten that among the fae, you had to be on your guard before their slyness cut you. "To save my brother from what?"

"From being a person who would kidnap a group of children and lead them to their deaths."

I opened my mouth, but just then Per froze and held up one hand.

And we all heard, very clearly, the sound of a child sobbing.

13

Anna's cane stuttered along the ground. Per tilted forward and sniffed the air before recalling himself and adopting a more human pose. The sound of crying stopped abruptly, leaving a heavy silence behind.

"Was it real?" Anna asked, after a moment.

"Yes," I said. "Faerie tricks are beautiful singing, or mirages of feasts, or merry parties. They understand what humans want, but not how humans feel. They would never think that a child's cry could get a reaction out of anyone."

"The cry is not a trick," Per said. "But there are other tricks ahead. Be careful, Princess."

I glanced at him, surprised. When the fae called me *Princess*, it was usually a gibe. But the rat prince said it respectfully.

"I'll be careful," I said. I strode ahead of him and Anna. Suddenly I was surrounded.

Tiny creatures filled the tunnel, like a waterfall of arrows. They streamed past me, over me, and around me, small and dizzyingly swift, filling my ears with high-pitched squeaks that bounced around the cave. I screamed and pulled in magic before I realized that nothing was touching me. Ghostly shadows dashed inches over my head and all around me, but not one brushed by me.

Bats.

A moment later they were gone, streaming down the tunnel ahead of us, a cloud of dark shapes melding with the blackness. My heart pounded so hard I was sure Per could hear it. I gripped my elbows with my hands, pressing my arms against my body.

"That wasn't *funny,*" I said.

"That wasn't *me.*" Per looked puzzled, then, after a moment, offended. "Why would you think it was me?"

The second *me* sounded more like a growl than he probably intended.

"She didn't!" Anna said hastily. "Right, Clare? She was just startled."

The rat prince stepped toward me. "Do you think bats are *rats?*"

"Aren't they?" I was not in the mood to be conciliatory. "Are you telling me that if rodents have wings, they are no longer your subjects? Because I don't believe—"

"Bats are not flying rats!" He was so infuriated he was losing control of his disguise; his teeth began to protrude and his skin looked fuzzy. "They're flying *monkeys*! They have nothing to do with me."

I glanced at Anna. She was staring at the rat prince in horror—whatever she could see of his face, it was enough for her to realize that he was no longer completely human. "I don't know," she said, in response to my look. "I don't know anything about bats."

Neither did I. But I didn't think the rat prince's outrage was faked. Besides, he wasn't upset that I had suspected him of attacking us, only that I had included bats among his subjects.

"All right," I said. "My apologies. But if you're not controlling the bats, then who is?"

"I don't think anyone is," Anna said. "They didn't hurt you, right? They just flew around you."

Easy for her to say.

"Someone must be drawing them in," the rat prince said. "Bats wouldn't normally go so deep into the caves. And they don't have a roost here—if they did, we'd smell it." His eyes narrowed. "Your brother is playing his pipe somewhere up ahead. That's what they hear."

He snapped his head sideways as he spoke, giving every impression of having ears that could tilt forward. We all stood silent, listening hard. But there was no sound except the faint, musical murmur of water dripping slowly down the sides of the tunnel.

"I don't hear anything," Anna said finally, sounding embarrassed.

"None of us do," I said. "Bats must be able to hear things humans can't."

"So can rats," Per said indignantly. "What makes you so sure *I* can't hear it, just because the two of you can't?"

"Because if you heard the pipe's music," I retorted, "you wouldn't still be standing here, would you?"

The corner of Per's mouth quirked upward. "Probably not. However, this does present a problem." He sent his glow light floating ahead, and I saw that just a few yards in front of us the passageway came to an end. We were in a small cave with rippling walls and broken-off stalactites. At the far end, past a twisted column that stretched from the ceiling to the ground, two passageways led in opposite directions.

Water hit my forehead. I glanced up at the slimy graygreen rocks overhead, then closed my eyes briefly and concentrated. It took me only a moment to feel Tom, less vaguely than before; our bond tugged me toward him urgently and unmistakably. Unfortunately, it pulled me straight in the direction of the jagged stone wall between the two passageways.

Our bond drew me toward Tom in a straight line.

Which, it turned out, was a lot less useful when an underground maze lay between us.

"Are we having a problem?" Per's smile revealed sharp teeth.

I turned from his smirk and peered down both passageways. There was no sign of which way the bats had gone. The one on the right looked like it curved downward, so I stepped into it. "This way."

"Are you sure?" Per said.

"No," I snapped, and strode forward.

I wasn't sure, but after a few yards, I was *pretty* sure. The glow light revealed a wide tunnel, with a fairly level floor and walls dripping with moss. Moss wouldn't grow in complete darkness, so this had to be a well-traveled route, by fae standards. Which meant we were probably getting somewhere.

So I had better focus on what I was going to do when I got *somewhere*. It was hard to think past finding Tom; part of me believed that all I needed was to get to him, and he would fix everything. But he probably wasn't expecting me to show up (1) at all, and (2) with two people who had ample reason to dislike him.

I wasn't too worried about Anna. Me and Tom, together, could more than handle her. But Per ... I had to do something about Per.

"Stop," Per said sharply.

I turned to look at him just as my foot plunged into ice-cold water.

I jumped back, water splashing up my leg. Ripples spread ahead as far as I could see before dying back into stillness. In front of me was a lake, the water so motionless that I could see the rock formations extending deep below.

"I guess this is the wrong way," Per said cheerfully. "The children are down the other passageway."

Too cheerfully. I knelt and skimmed my glow light along the surface of the water, which was so clear that I could easily see the tiny footsteps on the lake's floor. Dozens of them, overlapping and smudging each other.

"No," I said. "The children came this way." I reached up and broke off a narrow stalactite, then threw it toward the deepest rock column.

It hit the water in a series of ripples, then lodged in the mud just inches beneath the surface. The pond wasn't deep after all; the columns that looked like they extended far beneath the surface were actually just reflections of the stalagmites jutting out of the very shallow water.

"It's only a few inches deep," I said. "All the way across, looks like. Hope you don't mind getting wet."

Per made a tiny, growling sound. Since I wasn't facing him, I allowed myself a small smirk. Rats hate getting wet.

"No thanks," he said. "It will be a while before I follow a member of *your* family into water again. I'll find a way around this pond."

"How—" I began, then felt the magic surge from him. I turned as he finished the change, dropping to his front paws and lashing his tail against the ground.

"See you on the other side," he said, then dashed sideways and disappeared into a crevice in the rocks.

"Wait!" Anna said, but it was too late. He was gone.

"It's all right," I said. I didn't mean it—I felt weirdly defenseless without Per, but I knew that made no sense. "We don't need him to guide us. It was the other way around."

Anna frowned, still staring at the rocks Per had disappeared among.

"And anyhow," I said, "soon we'll be with Tom."

I *did* mean that, but Anna's frown didn't change. She leaned down and dipped a finger into the water. "Should we take off our shoes, or—"

A hand rose from the water, closed around her wrist, and pulled her in.

14

I was on my feet even before Anna splashed into the
water—so fast that I realized I had been expecting
something like this. In the Realms, stillness is never a
good sign.

Anna thrashed in the water, screaming, trying to
push herself up. Another hand reached for her hair,
pulling her down, and I saw that the hands weren't
emerging from the water—they *were* the water, taking
shape, forming limbs and heads and tails. Mermaids
made of water leapt at me, liquid and translucent, so
clear they were almost invisible. Their laughter echoed
off the rocks.

I reached for Anna, and cold, wet hands closed
around my wrists. They were shockingly strong; it was
like being pulled by a current. I reached for magic to
push back, but my power was like half an oar against a

waterfall. I slid into the water, my hands ripped from Anna's arms, my head hitting the base of a stalagmite.

I pushed against the bottom, but the force holding me down was relentless. The current around me bubbled with mirth, laughter muffled by the water. I hadn't had time to take a breath, and my lungs were already burning. . . .

But I knew what to do. Tom had taught me, after the sea serpent incident. If I could only remember . . .

Clare. The magic is still there, just different. His familiar calm, steely voice. *You have to let the water in.*

The water beside me wasn't swirling anymore; Anna was sprawled motionless at the bottom of the lake. Panic squeezed my throat and my brain. I had to breathe, I needed *air*, and it was so close, but I was being pushed down and I couldn't—couldn't—

Don't panic, Clare. Trust *me.*

I'd listened to him then. I'd done it once. I could do it again.

I opened my mouth and water rushed in. For a moment my mind went black, but I let the water down my throat, pulling magic with it, twisting it into the spell Tom had taught me—

—and drew in a breath. And then another.

Breathing underwater wasn't comfortable, even with the spell. It *hurt.* I had forgotten how much it hurt.

I let my body go limp on the rocky bottom, the water settling over me, so cold it numbed my skin. I couldn't tell the difference between the weight of the water and the press of the watery hands. I opened my eyes and saw Anna's body lying completely still.

I didn't know how to perform the breathing spell on another person. It probably wasn't even possible. But if I tried to grab Anna, the water-mer would realize I wasn't drowning, and they would find another way to kill me.

I breathed in more water, as subtly as I could, and barely noticed the pain. It hurt much more to think that Anna was going to die here and that I couldn't stop it. Even though she had tricked me, even though she was planning to trap Tom—

To trap Tom.

I twisted, as subtly and slowly as I could, and reached out with one hand. Luckily, I didn't have to reach very far, and even more luckily, I was on Anna's right side. I reached into her pocket, pulled out the iron bracelet, and poured as much magic into it as I could.

It blazed hot, burning my hand, making the water sizzle with heat and iron. The watery murmurs turned to screams as the iron touched the mer's translucent forms. They pulled back so sharply that Anna and I lay on dry rocks.

I grabbed Anna by the shoulders and pulled, trying to get her out of the pool. She was surprisingly heavy, but I had no time to use magic; I had to get her away from the water before the mer recovered. I yanked her so hard that I nearly fell over backward.

The water swirled and sloshed toward us, like a shallow ocean wave, forming a frothy circle around Anna's right foot. I pulled again, and the froth coiled tighter, becoming a white bubbling chain. Then her shoe came off, plopping into the water, and I pulled the rest of her out of the pool.

The lake roiled and hissed. Clear, liquid forms rose from it, shifting and viscous but maintaining the clear outlines of mermaids.

Anna convulsed and started coughing up water. I didn't know how to help her, so I hovered helplessly until she sat up. Her eyes were swollen and red. She put one hand to her throat, as if surprised to find herself breathing.

"Clare?" Her voice came out raspy. "What were those things?"

"Water-mer," I said. "They're mermaids who angered the queen. She turned them into water but left them with the memory of their true forms."

Anna wrapped her arms around herself. "And they can only escape by drawing others to their deaths?"

I blinked at her. "No. My mother doesn't allow for escape from her punishments. There's nothing that can change their fate."

"Then why do they do it?"

"They don't need a why. They're bored."

Anna touched one hand to her head, and I wondered if she was remembering the giggling mermaid in the lagoon who had amused herself by combing our hair. That same mermaid would have found it just as much fun to drag us under the water and watch us drown. Not that she would have; she'd have been too afraid of what Tom would do to her afterward.

I handed Anna the iron band. She looked at it, looked at me, then bit her lip and put it back in her pocket.

I touched a hand to her hair and dried it, then waved my other hand at her feet. Her single shoe disappeared and was replaced by a pair of elegant lavender slippers.

Anna drew in her breath, and only then did I dry myself. I wasn't sure why I was trying to impress her—pretty shoes wouldn't exactly make up for the fact that I had almost let her die—but for some reason, the awe on her face made me feel better.

"Faerie clothes aren't practical, but *these* are?" she said.

I giggled, a little harder than was called for. Then I had to use a bit of magic to make myself stop. "I guess not." I changed the slippers into boots like mine—sturdy and practical—but kept them lavender. "How's that?"

"Perfect," Anna said. "Thank you." She got to her feet, then put out her hand to catch herself on the wall. She squeezed her eyes shut, as if holding back tears, and her voice quavered. "Where's my cane?"

It had fallen and rolled under a ledge when she was pulled into the water. I retrieved it and handed it to her. The mer were as still as ice statues, glaring at us. I could see the bottom of the pool once again, as clearly as if there was no water there. The footprints had vanished. They had been a trick. The mer had heard us talking and showed us what they knew would draw us in.

"I guess we took the wrong turn." This time, I let my voice shake; it didn't seem fair, using magic to seem brave when Anna couldn't. "Let's go try the other passageway now."

———◆———

We were only five minutes down the other passageway when we heard the music.

We had seen no sign of Per, which was fine with me. I wasn't sure whether or not he had known the watermer were there; but if he had, he had obviously decided to give us to them, now that I had gotten him close enough to Tom. And if he hadn't known . . . well, we had certainly screamed loudly enough for him to hear us. Yet he hadn't come back.

Even though I had never trusted him, his betrayal made me angry. So stupidly human of me.

I wasn't sure whether Anna realized what Per had done. There was certainly no point in bringing it up; I wanted someone to share my anger with, but a small part of me was also angry at Anna for trusting him, which made even less sense than being angry at Per.

Even so . . . what if we came across Per again? Anna had to know better than to rely on him again. So I had to bring it up.

I had just opened my mouth when the soft, lilting sound of the pipe drifted down the tunnel, distorted by echoes and distance, but still long and sharp and achingly beautiful.

We both froze. Anna's lips parted, and my breath caught. Then, in unison, we broke into a run.

I felt the music through my skin almost as much as I heard it with my ears. An overwhelming, joyful eagerness filled me. For a second the curving rocks and uneven shadows around me vanished, and my head filled with a vision of huge yellow and purple flowers swaying in the breeze. I smelled wind and sunlight and magic.

Tom.

My head hit a stalactite, and the vision vanished. We were still in the passageway, and the music of the queen's pipe coiled through my blood, pulling me onward. I clenched my fists hard enough to hurt and forced myself to stop, to root myself to the ground and stand still.

Beside me, Anna flung her cane to the ground and danced past me. She held her arm out in front of her, forearm slanted diagonally, but she was moving so fast that she grunted with pain when her arm hit a wall. She used her hands to feel her way around the wall, then danced her way into the tunnel, her feet tapping and clumping on the rocky ground.

I bent to pick up the cane before I followed her.

I was so focused on the music ahead of me that I didn't hear the rustling and squeaking behind me. The rats came in a surge, hitting my ankles with their heavy, furry bodies. I shrieked and kicked at them, already pulling in magic to heal their bites. But no teeth sank into my skin; instead the rats were suddenly gone.

Bats followed a moment later. This time I didn't flinch as they filled the air with their thin, shrill chittering. None of them touched me. They weren't attacking me, and neither were the rats. I was just an obstacle for them to get around.

They streamed ahead of me, leaving the tunnel still and empty.

Anna cried out as the rats rushed past her, and I heard a thud as they knocked her off her feet. I reached her just as she stumbled upright, and I handed her the cane. She grabbed it and started tap-tapping, careless in her haste. Her feet hit the stump of a stalagmite and she fell again, her cane skittering across the floor. By the time I brought it to her, she was on her feet again and feeling the air in front of her with shaking hands.

"Here." I put the cane in one of her hands, then took the other. "I know it's hard, but don't rush. You have to be careful." I hesitated, then added, "Neither of us can see as well as a rat."

"I'm going to be too slow," Anna sobbed. "I'm going to be left behind."

"You won't," I said. "I'm right here with you. Just hold my hand."

Her fingers clutched mine. "I need light."

"Right. Sorry." I had stopped focusing on the glow light, and the tunnel had gone dim again. I poured magic into it until Anna held up one hand, telling me to stop. Then, together, we walked down the narrow, uneven passageway.

The music of the pipe wound through my bones, urging me forward. I had to force myself to obey my own instructions to Anna and walk at a steady pace. My pounding heart and my racing blood wanted me to run, to fly down the corridor with my arms outstretched, to dance my way to my brother. I knew, I *knew*, he was waiting to grab my hands and take me to safety. I could almost hear his low, confident laugh, almost taste the sparkling air of home.

But this wasn't my first enchantment. I knew how to resist, and I did, fighting the pull of the pipe and the yearning in my blood. It took me a few seconds, but then I was back in control.

Anna wasn't as experienced. She kept trying to pull away from me, her feet shuffling along the ground as she attempted to dance and run at the same time. It was irritating and uncomfortable, and I had to work on not yanking her back too hard. Finally, after I slipped on a loose rock and almost wrenched my arm out of its socket, I pulled my hand free and strode ahead of her. "Just follow me," I said over my shoulder. "Focus on walking. The fae can't really compel you to do anything you don't want to do."

"But I do want to," Anna said. "I want to dance. I want to go somewhere else, somewhere away from Hamelin and my father, somewhere beautiful. I want to be in the Realms."

I shook my head, though I knew she probably couldn't see it. "Just because the Realms are beautiful doesn't mean they're safe. Those children aren't being taken to the Realms to dance in meadows and ride magic water-falls."

"Why not?" Anna said. "That's what we did there."

Before I could reply, I slipped again. It wasn't just a loose rock this time; the whole corridor was slanting downward. I skidded forward on slick mud and pebbles, and then I heard the pebbles falling over the precipice ahead and clattering far below.

It took me a moment to realize I wasn't going to be able to stop sliding, and another moment to reach for magic. Which was a moment too many. I was able to slow my fall, but not to stop it, as I plunged over the precipice and down.

Behind me, Anna shouted my name. The air whistled past me, and I screamed.

Then, abruptly, there was only silence.

15

I opened my eyes to red-tinged blackness. The ground was rock-hard and covered with pebbles. A dull, reddish glow lit the rock formations far above me, and past them, I could see Anna's small white face peering down.

The reddish glow came with the scent of sulfur. So I wasn't surprised when I turned my head and saw a dragon coiled against a stalagmite several yards from me, its scales glowing like banked fire, its regular, heaving breaths filling the cave with drafts of warmth. It was asleep, but its huge eyelids flickered translucently, and it shifted its weight as I got to my feet.

"Clare?" Anna called. Judging by her despairing tone, it wasn't the first time she had said my name.

"Shhh!" I hissed. "I'm all right. Don't wake it."

"Clare? Can you hear me? What's that red glow?"

Great. She couldn't see me, and she probably wouldn't

hear me unless I yelled. But I was only yards away from the dragon's ears.

I crouched, picked up a small pebble, and threw it up as far as I could, aiming to the side of Anna's face. The pebble arced high in the air and fell straight back down. It looked like it was going to hit me, so I stumbled back, holding my hands over my head. The pebble landed several feet away from me, skittered sideways, and hit one of the dragon's claws.

Its eyes opened. It regarded me through gigantic black pupils in luminous red eyes. Then its eyelids flickered down again and it let out a rumbling snore.

"Clare!" Anna screeched, more loudly than before.

I sighed. "I'm here!" I shouted. "I'm all right. It's not too far down."

The dragon shifted, tucked its head under one claw, and went on snoring.

"Wait there!" Anna yelled. "I'm coming!"

"No, that's not what—"

Her cane clattered down next to me, hitting the ground in a spray of dirt and then rolling toward the dragon. It stopped a few inches from the dragon's side.

"Anna, wait—"

She was already climbing down. The climbing part lasted for only a few seconds before it was interrupted by a crack and a scream. I had just enough time to step forward and break her fall. She crashed into me, and we tumbled to the ground together.

Anna was lucky; she landed on top. She scrambled to her feet while I was still curled up wincing. "Where's my cane? Why is it so warm here? What's that red—"

"Keep your voice down," I hissed, even though there hardly seemed to be a point anymore. I got to my feet, retrieved her cane, and handed it to her. "We don't want to wake the dragon."

"The *what?*"

"Don't worry, it's asleep. For now." It suddenly occurred to me that when we weren't talking, the only sound was the dragon's soft snores. "What happened to the music? Where's Tom?"

I could see Anna wavering between answering me and pursuing the *dragon* issue. But something in my tone must have gotten through. "I didn't see Tom. The music stopped a short while after you fell."

I turned in a slow circle, my eyes adjusting to the red glow. We were in a small, shadowy cave. Green moss grew from the rocks, which told me that the dragon—and its glow—had been here for a while.

Nothing in my body hurt, which momentarily surprised me. I had gotten used to the way pain lingered outside the Realms.

It was a good reminder. I had been thinking like a

human. I had been trying to so I could manage in the human world. But it was time to start thinking like one of the fae again.

This cave wasn't a trap. If it was, there would be giant spiders or sucking quicksand or some sort of terrifying illusion. A large, sleeping dragon was nothing to the fae, nor was a leap into darkness.

I tugged at my bond with Tom and felt his presence, closer than before.

"It's all right," I said. "I think this is the way to the children."

"Uh-huh." Anna seemed very distracted by the dragon. "How do we get out of here before that thing wakes up? Can you fly us out?"

I sighed. "Don't sound so worried. Dragons aren't that bad, comparatively speaking."

"Compar—compared to *what*?"

"Well, you know. Mermaids. Or unicorns."

"Unicorns?"

"Even the most powerful fae are scared of unicorns." As I spoke, I used a bit of magic to untangle my hair and repair the rips in my dress. "In general, the more dangerous a magical creature is, the more gentle their reputation. They *want* humans to come near them. Though how unicorns ever managed to convince humans they were peaceful with those huge, sharp horns on their heads, I'll never know. I mean, what did you think the horns were for? Playing ring toss?"

"Enough about unicorns," Anna said through gritted teeth. "Can we talk about dragons? Specifically, about the dragon that is awake and glaring at us right now?"

I turned. The dragon was watching us, its eyes so vividly red I wasn't surprised that Anna had noticed them. It opened its mouth, and a tiny puff of orange flame shot between its teeth and sputtered out.

"It's fine," I said, though I took a step back as I said it. Dragons didn't usually breathe fire unless they were angry. "Dragons are all tame these days. You can just treat it as if it were a dog."

"I'm afraid of dogs!"

"Why would you be afraid of a dog?" I said incredulously. "They don't even breathe fire."

"But they bite!"

"Well, you don't have to worry about that. Dragons don't bite. They only use their teeth *after* they've burned their prey to a crisp."

Anna made a strangled sound.

The dragon closed its eyes again and settled its head on its front claws. I watched it until I was pretty sure it was asleep again, and then I called up a glow light.

I didn't dare make it too bright, so it probably didn't help Anna much. But even by the faint glow, I could clearly see the sides of the cave—and the spot where, right past the dragon's front claws, the stone walls curved into a pitch-black tunnel. I walked over and peered into the passageway, the dragon's glow heating my skin, then glanced back at Anna. "Let's go."

Anna blinked. In the light, I saw streaks on her cheeks.

She had been crying.

"Anna?" I bit my lower lip. "I'm sorry."

She looked at me, blinking rapidly—in her case, a sign that her eyes were getting tired. "For what?"

"You must have been really scared," I said awkwardly, "when I fell."

She nodded.

"But I don't think you would have been trapped here. Tom would have found you. . . ." My voice trailed off. Would Tom really have done anything for her? The only person he had ever taken care of was me.

"You dolt," Anna said. "I was scared for *you*! I thought you had died!"

"Oh," I said distractedly. I was thinking about my brother, who had protected and cared for me, had told me stories and guided me through dangerous places, but had never shown a hint of concern for anyone else. And who was now in charge of a bunch of helpless human children. "Well, I'm all right."

Anna muttered something under her breath, then came to stand next to me, sweeping her cane cautiously in front of her.

I peered into the narrow, upward-sloping tunnel. "It looks clear to me," I said. "This must lead to where Tom and the children are."

Okay, *must* was a strong word. But Anna didn't question it. When I stepped into the tunnel, she was right behind me. Maybe she finally trusted me.

More likely, she just wanted to get away from the dragon.

The sides of the passageway narrowed, and I hunched my shoulders as I walked between them, ducking occasionally so as not to hit my head on low-hanging rocks. There was no moss on the pitted gray walls, which made me think this tunnel wasn't the normal way to get to . . . wherever we were going. But my sense of Tom's nearness got stronger with every step. We were definitely headed in the right direction.

When we reached the end of the passageway, the opening was covered by spiderwebs so thick that they hung from the top of the cave in lacy white veils. But after only a few seconds of ripping through them, I stepped out into a large, airy chamber.

The ground here was nearly flat, the ceiling a series of curves and ridges that narrowed into black crevices. The walls were covered with green moss and also with rust-red lines, giving the impression of a vast, elaborate tapestry. Stalactites hung low above us, curving together like chandeliers, magical light flickering through and around them. The lights were tiny, but there were so many of them that they illuminated the whole cavern.

The Underground Ballroom. I had heard of this place; the fae loved to reminisce about the parties they'd once had here. But the point of those parties had been to ensnare humans, so none had been held since the Pact.

The cavern was so silent I could hear the distant murmur of water on stone, and the soft, steady breathing of dozens of sleeping children. Sleeping, living children. They lay on the floor, curled up in groups, eyes closed. Some rested their heads on bunches of moss that they'd formed into pillows. Others lay with their heads on each other's stomachs or pillowed on their own arms. Most of the younger ones seemed perfectly comfortable sprawled on the ground.

I let out a breath of relief when I saw that there still *were* younger ones. In the few days the children had been gone, they might have grown older than their parents. That was a possibility I had avoided mentioning to Anna.

But we were in luck. (Well, by some definition of the word *luck*.)

Anna made strangled sounds of disgust as she tried to peel fragments of spiderweb from her hair. I reached for magic—the cave was full of it—and removed all the spiderwebs from both of us. Then I looked past the sleeping children. The walls arced upward in a series of uneven ridges and rock formations; there was plenty of space in those dark crevices for someone to hide.

But Tom had never been one for hiding.

I walked across the open space. The wall curved, so with each step, more of the ballroom became visible. I had almost reached the first cluster of sleeping children when I saw him.

A thick gray stalagmite jutted up from the ground, uneven bumps and veins bulging from its sides. A lanky boy balanced easily on its flat top, one knee up near his chin, the other leg dangling against the rock. He turned his head as I approached.

He looked exactly the same: long narrow face, deep bright eyes, a hint of a smile curving his thin lips upward. His hair was longish, which hid the fact that when it was short, his ears stuck out. He lifted an eyebrow at me, as if to say, *What took you so long?*

"Hello, Tom," I said.

16

"Clare," Tom replied. His voice was perfectly calm; no one but me would have realized that he was surprised. And even I couldn't tell if he was angry. "What are you doing here?"

I had been thinking for weeks about what I would say to my brother when we finally met again. I had a bunch of zingers polished and memorized, to let him know how angry I was. I'd thought about being cold and calm, showing him that all this time, I hadn't needed him after all. I'd been pretty sure that, no matter what I rehearsed, I would end up just throwing myself at him and hugging him.

Instead, the first thing I said to my brother was, "She's looking for you."

Tom did not have to ask who *she* was. He straightened, every line of his body taut. "How close?"

"She opened the portal into the caves for me." I

swallowed, suddenly seeing her assistance the way he might: as me betraying him. But his steady gaze didn't change. "She already knew you were here. I think she's angry at you."

"Of course she's angry at me," Tom said. "I'm late with her children."

My heart stuttered. I looked around at the sleeping children, and then at my brother. "Why, Tom?"

"Why am I late? I ran into an unexpected snag." Tom lowered his other leg and leaned back on his hands. "I'm hiding out for a bit while I figured out how to solve it. But apparently I just ran out of time."

"I'm sorry," I said. "I didn't know—" I stopped short. Why was *I* apologizing? "Why did you steal the children? Did the queen order you to?"

If she had, that would make sense. Tom couldn't disobey an order from the queen. None of the fae could, and he was practically fae. Maybe he was obeying the compulsion reluctantly, trying to find a way . . .

But he shook his head before my hope could fully form. "She didn't command me. We have an agreement about what she'll give me in exchange for them."

"An agreement? You mean this is part of some *bargain*?" I looked at the children again. Their breathing was soft and peaceful—unnaturally so; the music we'd heard earlier had been Tom putting them to sleep. "What could you possibly have bargained for in exchange for *this?*"

"Something worth it," he said, with a mysterious smile.

"Nothing could be worth it!" But even as I said it, I knew it wasn't true. Not to him.

And the worst thing was that I wasn't even surprised. I looked at his cold fae eyes, the self-satisfied curve of his lips, and saw nothing I hadn't seen a hundred times before. Seen and ignored, or told myself was camouflage, or not questioned at all. By the standards of the Realms, there was nothing cruel or surprising about what Tom was doing.

Out in the human world, I hadn't wanted to believe Tom was capable of kidnapping the children. But here in the Realms, staring at his impish fae grin and the familiar sparkle in his eyes, I knew that he was. Of course he was. None of the fae would even hesitate.

Had I honestly thought that all I had to do was show up and remind him that kidnapping was wrong? Or at least, that *I* really didn't want him to kidnap children, so could he please let them go to make his little sister feel better?

I took a deep breath. It was, still, the only plan I had.

I stepped toward him, marshaling my arguments, all the points I'd rehearsed over and over on my way to find him.

That was when I heard the scamper of claws somewhere high above us.

I had just enough time to look up—but not enough to scream a warning—before the rat prince launched himself from one of the rock ledges, flew through the air, and landed on Tom's shoulders.

Tom fell forward off his perch, a giant rat clinging to his back. He hit the ground, rolled, and kicked. The creature that flew away from him was in human form, pale-faced and blue-eyed, showing human teeth as he snarled.

Tom leapt to his feet, then leapt again, farther than was humanly possible. He landed on the far wall of the cavern. Magic surged from him as he scrambled straight up the wall, then launched himself onto another ledge. He reached overhead, broke off a stalactite, and threw it at the rat prince as if it was a spear.

Per dodged and scrambled up a nearby wall. The stalactite hit the ground and shattered. Children woke up screaming as its shards flew everywhere; they sat up and stared around in confused, bleary terror. One little boy began to cry.

"Get back, children!" Anna called. "Come to me, quick! Into this passageway."

The rat prince leapt onto a ledge across from Tom's. He broke off a stalactite of his own and flung it across the space between them. Tom threw himself onto his stomach, and the makeshift weapon flew right above his prone body and shattered in the dim recesses behind him.

Tom leapt into a crouch and raised one hand. Silver flashed between his fingers. He lifted the pipe to his lips, and a clear, shivering tune rang through the cave.

The children froze. So did Anna, in the act of herding them. At exactly the same second, they all lifted their faces toward Tom and his pipe.

I could feel the magic in the pipe, and that vision of purple and yellow flowers flashed through my mind again. This time, it took me only a moment to shrug it off. The rat prince merely sneered as he reached behind him and wrenched another stalactite from the wall.

Then the pipe's tune rose, so high it hurt my ears, and the ledge Per was standing on crumbled and fell right out from under him.

His scream, as he plummeted, sounded like an animal's.

The pipe's music stopped short, and the spell broke.

Several of the children shrieked. The rat prince landed and whirled, a blur of brown. He dashed in a furry streak across the cavern and into one of the crevices along the wall.

"Tom!" I shouted. "He's going to come up behind you!"

My brother lifted an eyebrow—*Do you think I don't know that?*—before he somersaulted off the ledge, flipped in midair, and landed lightly right next to me.

"Show-off," I muttered.

He grinned. Then he put his back to mine and we circled slowly, searching the walls and ceiling for any sign of the rat prince.

It was an impossible task. The cavern was full of narrow crevices and dark spaces, and Per could have been in any of them, completely invisible to us until he came plummeting down. On the farther end of the cavern, past Tom's perch, a jagged crack ran along the ground: a crevice in the earth. I knew from experience that anything could be hiding down there. I pulled in magic, holding it ready.

"Why does he want the children?" I asked, glancing sideways. Anna still had them gathered near the mouth of the tunnel, all wide eyes and terrified pale faces.

"*He* doesn't," Tom said tersely. "He was supposed to help me bring them to the queen. Now he's afraid he'll be punished for my failure."

"Why does *our mother* want them?"

"She didn't tell me."

I wished I could see Tom's expression. There was something odd in his voice. Not that I thought Tom would lie to me, but he wasn't telling me the whole truth. "Didn't you *ask*, before you made your bargain?" I demanded. "Or did you not care enough to even wonder?"

Tom stopped circling. I turned and met his dark eyes. His face was taut, a pattern of lines and angles, and the sharpest angle of all was the one his jaw made as he regarded me.

"She would not have explained," Tom said. "She never does when she sends me on missions among the humans. It's always 'stick a sword in a stone,' or 'grow that beanstalk into the sky,' or 'turn some princes into swans.'" He shrugged. "It's not like I ever ask why."

And not like he ever objected, either.

"But you can guess, can't you?" I asked. "What do you *think* our mother is going to do to these children, Tom, if you hand them over to her?"

Tom bit his lip, then whirled and lashed out with his magic.

He caught the rat prince in mid-spring. Per screamed. There was a sizzle, the scent of burning fur, and then a sickening thud as Per hit the ground. When he scrambled to his feet, he was in human form, though his snarl revealed teeth too sharp to be human.

"Thought we were distracted, did you?" Tom was still smiling, but grimly. He lifted his pipe to his lips and played a few jaunty notes, with more force behind them than before. Per's body jerked and he began to dance, his legs and arms flailing stiffly, his dark eyes glaring at us.

This time, I had my guard up, so the pipe didn't affect me. Pebbles skittered behind us, and I whirled. The children were dancing, too, and so was Anna, her expression frantic and trapped.

"Tom," I said. "Stop."

"Why?" Tom said. "They're pretty good dancers."

He was laughing, his lips curved around the mouthpiece of the pipe, his fingers moving expertly over the holes. For a moment, I saw him the way Anna must see him: too carelessly wild to be human, thin and wiry, and very, very dangerous.

"It's not right," I said. The words felt foreign on my tongue. "You're ... you're taking away their free will. Let them go. Please."

Tom gave me an irritated look, but he stopped playing, ending with a long, shrill note that froze everyone in place. Per's legs snapped together and his arms stuck to his sides, his eyes practically bulging from their sockets with the intensity of his glare. There was no doubt that if he *could* have moved, he would have ripped Tom's throat out, even with human teeth.

"Keep dancing!" a child wailed behind us. "I like the dancing."

"I can't move, you nincompoop!" another child snapped.

"I can't move either!"

"Don't call me a nincompoop!"

"Hush," Anna said, her voice strained. She had frozen in an awkward position, half bending toward one of the children, and looked like she was about to fall over.

"Tom," I said, "can you—"

He motioned me into silence. "Well," he said to the rat prince. "This is awkward."

"Not really," Per growled. "You can't hold me here forever."

"Can't I?" Tom said.

"You're *human*." I had heard that word snarled as an insult a million times. But not directed at Tom, not for a very long while. "You'll run out of patience long before I do. How many years have you lived—thirty? Forty?"

Seventeen. Not that it mattered.

Per jerked one arm upward. Tom blew a quick note, and Per froze again, but he smirked. "I'm more powerful than you think."

"Yes," Tom said thoughtfully, "you are. Why is that?"

"Because *I* am still obeying the queen's wishes. Here in the Realms, that matters." Per's eyebrows got bushier as they arced together above his nose. "You won't find it easy to thwart her will *here*, even with the pipe you stole from her."

"I didn't steal it," Tom said. "She gave it to me."

"She gave it to you," Per said, "so you could bring her the children. Instead you've chosen to gather them here." He bared his teeth. "I don't know why you would disobey the queen, or how you thought you could get away with it. But I won't let you drag me into your rebellion."

"It's not a rebellion," Tom snapped. "I can't bring her the children yet. She asked for *all* of them, and I'm missing some."

My breath caught, but neither of the princes glanced at me. Hopefully, they were too distracted to have heard me. I managed to keep from looking at Anna, who was still frozen in place.

"If I don't bring them all," Tom said, "she's going to claim I haven't fulfilled my part of the bargain. I was trying to figure out how to get the rest of them when *you* came along and started annoying me." He played another tune. There was a cracking sound from above, and I glanced up. But whatever was breaking in the ceiling of the cavern, it was too high and hidden to see.

"I don't care about your bargain," Per growled. "I care about the queen's anger. You made me part of this plan, and now I'm going to see it through. Give me the pipe, and I'll bring *these* children to the queen."

"I don't think so." Tom blew a shrill, shivering note on the pipe, so dissonant I had to cover my ears. Per, who didn't have the ability to cover his ears, snarled in pain.

Something small and brown leapt through the air in front of me. I shrieked and drew back, and the rat collided with Tom's pipe, knocking it out of his hand.

Tom swore and lunged, but another rat had already dashed out from beneath a stone ledge and grabbed the silver pipe between its teeth. It ran across the cavern floor, its odd, bouncing gait accentuated by the weight of the pipe.

Tom flung out one hand. A surge of magic crackled through the cavern—but it was shattered by another, stronger blast of power, this one from Per. Their magic met and exploded, sending power ricocheting against the walls. Several rock formations broke off and shattered to the ground, and another groaning, ominous crack sounded above us. Stones crumbled into the crevice, falling a very long way before crashing distantly far below.

The two small rats streaked across the cavern floor, straight toward Per. He laughed triumphantly and knelt, holding his hand out for the pipe.

He had completely forgotten about me.

I drew in more magic and lashed out with it. This magic came from the battle between the two princes, and it was a wild and violent power. I didn't have a hope of controlling it, and I didn't try to. I just threw it at Per and his rats and the pipe.

All three of them flew backward, right toward the crevice in the earth.

Everyone was screaming now: the children, Anna, me. Per roared, and his rats squealed in terror, and the silver pipe fell from the thief's mouth and rolled across the floor toward the crevice.

Tom was the only one not screaming. But I heard his gasp, somehow loud even in the chaos, as the pipe teetered at the edge of the chasm—

And fell.

Tom and Per dove for it at the same time. They were both too late. There was a series of thunks as the pipe bounced down the walls.

Then there was only the children's screaming and sobbing.

The rat that had dropped the pipe turned and ran, disappearing into a crack in the wall. Per watched it go, then turned his cold eyes on Tom.

"Well," he said. "*Now* it's awkward."

17

Behind me, the children were in hysterics, screaming and crying and, for some reason, hitting each other. Anna was frantically and futilely trying to calm them. She sounded pretty close to hysterics herself.

In front of me, the two princes stood glaring at each other. For the first time I noticed how similar they looked: the same coiled pose, the same cold eyes.

"I do believe this ends our partnership," Per said. "I look forward to telling the queen that you not only stole her children but also lost her pipe."

"It's not lost," Tom snapped. "It can be retrieved. It just takes some courage."

My head snapped up. Tom didn't glance at me—his eyes were fixed on Per's—but I knew that had been a signal. He had said those words to me so often, whenever something in the Realms seemed too strange or dangerous or treacherous for me to handle. *You can do it, Clare. It just takes some courage.*

"Is that what you call it?" Per sneered. "Defying the queen like this? You've overplayed your hand, Prince."

"No, I haven't," Tom said. "I'm just making sure I *complete* the task. You may not want to help me anymore, but fortunately, I don't need you."

"Don't you?" The rat prince gnashed his teeth, apparently forgetting that they were currently human teeth. "You don't seem to be doing all that well, *Your Highness*. You can't get all these children to follow you anywhere without the pipe. I'd say you're stuck."

"Believe that if you want." Tom stepped backward, and I realized what he was doing. Distracting Per and leading him away from the crevice.

I stepped forward, trying not to make a sound, and peered down into the crack in the ground. It was pitch black. I couldn't see how far down it went or what it contained.

I didn't have much time to think. Any moment now, Per would notice me. I remembered the time a sea serpent had grabbed me and pulled me underwater, and Tom dove in right after me, following me deeper and deeper into the murky depths.

Even though he didn't know how to swim.

It just takes some courage.

I didn't want to go into that dark crevice. Every muscle in my body clenched at the thought, every instinct in my brain screamed that I shouldn't. But Tom had never needed *me* before.

I shut off my mind and jumped.

The rat prince whirled, and I got a momentary glimpse of his face. Just long enough to see that he didn't look surprised at all. He looked *smug*.

I realized why as soon as I reached for magic to slow my fall.

It wasn't there.

I fell like a stone, a scream ripping from my throat. Per's smirk was seared into my mind. If it had been my first time without magic, I would have died.

But I had been in the human world for weeks now. I reached out with instincts I hadn't had a month ago, scrabbling desperately at the sides of the crevice, clawing for some sort of handhold.

And finding one.

My fingers closed around a jutting rock and I jolted to a stop, my body slamming against the stone wall. The rock I had grabbed was large and sturdy, but my momentum was so great that my fingers started sliding off it. I shoved my feet against the side of the crevice, gasping with relief when they landed on something solid—a slim ledge barely wide enough for my toes. I ran my other hand along the side of the wall and managed to wedge my fingers into a crack, just before the rock I had grabbed broke off. It bounced against the sides of the crevice several times, then shattered far below.

Very far below.

I clung to the wall with one hand, my body pressed to the bumpy stone wall, my legs braced against the ledge. Above me I could see a crack of light, but around me was nothing but darkness. My free hand slid futilely across rock, searching for a handhold and finding none.

"Clare!" Tom shouted, and a circle of light separated itself from the sliver of white above me. A glow light, swirling white and gray. It floated down and hovered above my head, giving me enough light to see a dip in the rock right above me. I grabbed the dip with my free hand and put my face against the rock, almost sobbing with relief.

Then I heard something skitter on the wall below me, coming up.

"Tom!" I screamed, and he sent the glow light closer to me.

It immediately went out.

The skittering got louder. Something furry brushed my foot. Far above, the rat prince laughed.

Teeth sank into my ankle.

I kicked with such force that I almost knocked myself loose. But I dislodged the rat, which squealed as it fell and then went abruptly silent.

Claws clicked on stone as more rats climbed up toward me.

I choked on a sob and looked up again. The opening above was filled with bright white light, but where my hands clutched the stone, it was pitch black. I couldn't see if there were any other handholds I could use to climb up. I might be able to feel for them . . . but that would mean abandoning my current grip. The very thought made me freeze up with fear. I was sure that if I made the slightest movement, I would fall.

Below me, the rats got louder. If they swarmed me, I would fall for sure.

I drew in a breath to scream. Before I could let it out, Tom was there, diving into the chasm with one hand stretched toward me.

"Don't!" I shouted. "There's no magic here!"

He halted sharply in midair. A glow light swirled above his shoulder, illuminating his wide eyes and taut jaw. "Where does the magic end?"

"Send the light first," I gasped. "It will go out when it crosses the border."

Tom nodded and let the light sink slowly.

I glanced down. By the grayish, swirling light, I could see a vast, scrabbling movement advancing up the stone. *"Faster."*

Tom grinned. He reached out and, with a quick wrench, yanked a segment of rock free. He hefted it and threw it right at the army of rats.

The rock shattered, raining down boulders and dirt, knocking the top rats loose. They squealed and flailed as they tumbled backward, crashing into the rats below them, causing a loud, furry avalanche that cascaded into the darkness.

"Not everything requires magic, little sister." Tom was following the glow light down as it descended, his cloak billowing around him. "I thought I taught you that."

The glow light went out, plunging us into darkness again. Tom made a "hmm" sound and called up another one.

"Although," he added, "magic *can* come in useful." He turned upside down carefully, his cloak falling past his head, and extended one hand toward me. His arm crossed the border, but he kept the rest of his body in the circle of light.

I had to let go entirely in order to grab his hand. I didn't hesitate. I braced my feet against the tiny ledge and jumped.

My fingers slid across Tom's and away. They closed on thin air, and I screamed. Then his other hand clamped around my wrist, and he yanked up so hard that he almost wrenched my shoulder out of its socket.

Magic surrounded me as soon as he pulled me up, but Tom didn't let go, and I didn't try to fly on my own. I closed my fingers around his wrist, letting the rest of my body go limp. Despite the distance below me and the squeaking of the rats, I felt no fear as I let my brother pull me over the precipice and into the questionable safety of the shadowy, magic-filled underground ballroom.

18

Tom pulled me onto solid ground, keeping hold of my hand. His grip was so tight it hurt, but I didn't complain. I pressed against his side as we turned to face the rat prince.

"That," Tom said to Per, "was a mistake."

I glanced over my shoulder. The children were all staring wide-eyed, as if at a fascinating puppet show. Anna had both fists pressed to her mouth.

"It's all right," I called to her. "I'm safe now."

Tom followed my gaze. For some reason, he smirked at Anna before focusing on me. "You've surprised me, Clare. I never expected you to try to find me, or to succeed in doing so. We'll have a lot to talk about once this is over."

Warmth expanded my chest. I smiled at him.

"That will be fun," I said. "Maybe I can go on your missions with you, after we bring the children back home."

Per snorted. "Nice try, Princess," he said. "But you can't get all these children back across the border without the pipe. And you can't get the pipe without the help of my subjects."

"No," Tom agreed, faintly regretful. "I suppose we'll have to leave the children here."

Anna made a choked noise. I looked over my shoulder again. Right away, I spotted the two children from the chalk drawing their mother had pressed into my hand, wide-eyed and clinging to each other. They both had shockingly bright red hair, which the black-and-white drawing hadn't revealed.

I resisted the urge to smile at them—after all, they had no idea who I was—and turned to my brother instead. "We can't leave the children here, Tom."

"Why not? I'll play music. I'll summon cakes. They'll love it here." He turned around to face Anna and the children. As he did, the colors on his clothes brightened. I couldn't see his face, but some of the children smiled tentatively back at him.

"What do you think?" he asked. His voice was smooth and almost musical, reminiscent of his piping. "Would you like to dance again, the way we did before? Remember how fun it was?"

A little girl giggled and wiped her cheeks dry. Around her, small heads nodded.

Wow. Who would have imagined it? Tom was *good* with children.

Although, he was cheating. Magic came off him in waves, making my heartbeat slow down and a calm, peaceful anticipation fill my chest. I fought it instinctively before remembering: this was Tom. I didn't have to fight anymore.

"What kind of cakes?" the red-haired boy demanded. He looked about five years old, or maybe ten. (I'm not good with human ages.) His hair was cropped close against his head, but still managed to have half a dozen leaves stuck to it. "I like chocolate."

His sister, whose hair was long and plastered over her face, turned and hit him. "I *hate* chocolate! You know I hate chocolate!"

"There will be many kinds of cake!" Tom promised. "As many as there are colors on my clothes! Can you count how many there are?"

The two went momentarily silent as they started counting colors. I gave Tom a sharp look. The humans might not realize it, but he was mocking them. There were hundreds of colors on his cloak, fae colors as well as human ones, hues and shades they could never see.

He widened his eyes at me innocently, and I sighed and shook my head.

"No," Anna said. Her voice was thin and high-pitched.

"You can't do this." Tom looked at her blankly, and she turned to me. *"Clare."*

I shook off my sense of happy contentment. "Tom. She's right."

"They'll be fine," Tom said impatiently. "I'll come back every few days and replenish their food."

No, I thought, *you won't.* The fae always forgot.

"I don't like *any* kinds of cake!" another girl wailed. "I want *pie*!"

"There will also be pie," Tom assured her.

"Tom!" I snapped. "Their parents want them back."

Tom swirled his cloak so the children could see the lining, which had even more colors. "Then their parents should have taken better care of them."

"How?" I said. "By paying you money they didn't have?"

"What are you talking about?" Tom said. "I didn't ask them for money."

"What *kind* of pie?" the red-haired boy demanded.

"You are focusing on the wrong thing," Tom said.

"Which of us are you talking to?" I demanded.

The anti-cake girl began sobbing again, her cries quickly escalating into a wail. I recognized it: hers was the cry Anna and I had heard in the caves, before we went down the wrong tunnel.

A muscle jumped in Tom's neck. "Look, it doesn't

matter. I can't take all of them back without the pipe. And I've had about enough of children. The little ones are constantly . . . *oozing* things. And it always seems to be my job to take care of it."

I raised an eyebrow. I knew him too well to believe that.

"Well," he amended, "it's my job to tell one of the older ones to take care of it."

"How very trying."

"Now that you're here, it will, of course, be your job."

"Why should it be *my* job?"

"It hardly seems fair to make the children keep doing it."

"If you're going to talk about *fair*—" I began, then recognized Tom's calm, eminently reasonable tone, which he always used to irritate me. And to distract me. I narrowed my eyes.

"I mean it, Tom," I said. "They don't belong here. They'll be better off at home."

"I don't care where the children will be better off," Tom said, in the same tone of voice he might have used for, *I don't care if you wear the purple sash or the blue one.*

(Actually, he would have cared about that.)

I stood looking at my brother, and the few feet between us felt like several leagues. I thought about crossing that space and taking his hand. I thought about asking him to take me to the Realms, where I would never think again about what he did when he was sent to the human world. We would be together, and we would be where we belonged, and I would forget the human world and its children.

Anna stepped toward Tom, and I tensed, remembering the iron band she had brought with her.

But all she did was look up at my brother, her face blankly intent, the way it got when she was straining to see. She wasn't that far from Tom, but the flickering lights made it difficult even for me to read his expression.

"Don't do it," she said. "Don't take them. Please. I . . ." Her voice cracked. "I'm sorry."

Tom didn't even bother to look at her. He smiled at me and held out one hand.

My stomach tightened. I had left the Realms to find Tom, and I'd found him. We were together again. A few weeks ago, I had thought that would be enough.

I wished I had never crossed the border, never heard about the children, never come to Hamelin. I wished this could all be happening without my knowing about it.

But it was too late for that.

"Find a way," I said to Tom. "If you really cared, you would find a way to get the pipe and bring them home."

Tom's shoulders twitched. "I told you. I *don't* really care."

"I know." And I did know, now. The knowing was a deep, painful ache inside me. "But *I* care, Tom."

My brother looked at me quizzically. The ache got heavier. I had told myself Tom wouldn't steal children, and that had been a lie. Then I had told myself he would do the right thing for my sake. Time to find out if that was a lie, too.

I was desperately, sickeningly afraid that it was. But I spoke anyhow. My voice shook so much it was almost unintelligible, but I could tell he understood. He always understood me. "I came here to bring the children back. Please, Tom. I'm begging you. Please help me bring them home."

His expression didn't change. I took a deep breath.

"Because if you don't take them," I said, "you're not taking me, either. I won't leave these caves without them."

19

The silence echoed through the cavern, long and agonizing. I felt tears gathering behind my eyes and fought them off. I had never before cared whether *Tom* saw me cry, but everything felt different now, like something in our bond had cracked. Like something I had thought would last forever was about to shatter.

So I knew that the worst thing I could do was cry. Because you never, ever cried in front of the fae.

Tom had never looked more fae than he did now, the lines of his face accentuated by the light from the stalactite chandeliers, his eyes dark and unfathomable. Seconds slid by with no indication that he was going to answer me, and I felt the crack deepen and break.

The red-haired girl picked up a piece of fallen stalactite and threw it at the red-haired boy. It hit him in the shoulder. He launched himself at her and tackled her to the ground, and they rolled over, screaming and flailing.

None of the other children reacted. I got the impression they had seen this many times before. But the two were so engaged in their fight that they did not seem to notice the crack in the ground.

Or the fact that they were rolling right toward it.

I sprinted over and pulled the children apart. One tiny fist hit me in the eye.

"Stop it!" I shouted. "Or there will be NO CAKE."

"Good!" the girl said. "I don't *like* cake!"

"But I do!" the boy screamed. "You're so selfish."

"*You're* so selfish!"

"You're selfisher!"

I dragged them farther from the precipice. In the process, I got kicked twice and punched again.

Once we were at a safe distance, I dropped them and stepped away. Instead of lunging at each other again, the girl crumpled to the ground sobbing, and the boy glared at me as if it were *my* fault.

I turned back to Tom, pretty sure my ultimatum had lost its intensity. Tom had moved back to the top of his pillar. I understood why. Per, too, had sidled farther away from the group of children.

"Can't you do something about them?" I demanded. "With magic?"

Tom shook his head. "If magic could be used to get children to behave, the humans would never have given it up. There would be no Pact." He raised an eyebrow. "And I guess we wouldn't be having this problem."

Of course we wouldn't. None of this would be happening if not for the Pact.

"Tom," I said, "why does our mother want the children?"

"I told you. She didn't inform me."

"She didn't inform me, either," Per said.

I shot him a glare.

"Not that I would tell you if she had." He shrugged. "It just seemed worth pointing out."

I turned my back on him. "You keep saying she didn't tell you," I said to Tom. "But you haven't said you don't know."

He threw his head back and laughed. "Very good, Clare. I wouldn't say I *know*, but I can guess." He hopped down from the pillar, landing lightly as a cat. "The Pact keeps the fae from crossing to the human world in their true form, and from using magic there. But it doesn't stop humans from crossing. Our mother misses meddling in the human world. That's why she's been sending me on missions so often. I think she figures if one human child is so useful, why not pick up some more?"

"But why a whole *town's children*?" Anna cut in. "I

never . . . I don't understand that part. It seems like over-doing it."

Tom met my eyes. I tried not to laugh. *Overdoing it* was how the fae did things.

"Every couple of years the occasional stray human passes the border," Tom said. "They're confused and lost, or sometimes"—his voice sharpened—"they're willing fools. Mostly, they die. They fall into a trap, or anger the wrong creature, or get lost and starve. My sister is right about how dangerous the Realms are."

Anna's chin went up, tight and trembling.

"If she starts out with dozens of children, though, she'll end up with a few who manage to stay alive." Tom glanced at the children, most of whom were still watching us. A couple had apparently gotten bored with the discussion of their fate and started kicking pebbles at each other. "That's why she gave me the pipe. With so many children, we can't count on all of them being willing. And the pipe is the only object of power we still possess that can draw humans between worlds." His gaze moved to the chasm. "With the rat prince's help, I devised a plan. It would have worked, too, except some of the children got left behind. I was going to fig-ure out a way to get them, but without the pipe . . ." He shrugged. "I think it's time to give the whole thing up."

"The queen will be rather angry," Per warned.

"I'll be all right," Tom said. "I have my sister to help me now."

I blinked at him, and he grinned at me. "You've grown up, Clare. Look at you, surviving in the human world, outmaneuvering His Rattiness here, and finding me. I think it's time we had an adventure of our own. A long, faraway one, to give Mother time to get over"—he waved a hand vaguely around the cavern—"all this."

A spark lit in me. I had begged Tom for years to take me with him on one of his adventures. He'd always said it was too dangerous. But then my gaze landed on a small, curly-haired boy, his thumb in his mouth.

"No," I said. "I told you, I'm not leaving without them."

Tom rolled his eyes. "Don't be stubborn."

"I'm not being stubborn! I mean, I *am* being stubborn." I crossed my arms over my chest. "How could you, Tom? After what the fae did to us. How *could* you do the same to other innocent children?"

"Stubborn *and* histrionic. Lovely." Tom sighed. "I'm not hurting them, Clare. They'll be safer in the Realms."

"No one's safe in the Realms!"

"And you think the human world is safe?" Tom ran a hand through his hair. "These humans are all *poor*, Clare. All it takes is a bad harvest, or a plague of rats, and they're in as much danger as they would be in the

Realms. Even when times are good, they don't have much to look forward to. They have nothing to go back to but a life of endless drudgery." His eyes flicked sideways. "Tell her, Anna. I know *you* agree with me."

Anna stared at him as if she were still frozen. Per looked from her to me to Tom, his expression bright with interest.

I remembered the streets of Hamelin, dour and gray. The grief in the air, so thick I had breathed it in and out with every step.

"They do have something to go back to," I said. "They have parents who love them."

"And in the Realms, they'll have each other. Like you had me. You don't know how good your life has been, Clare. You've never been hungry or cold. You've never been forced to endure hunger, or itchy clothes, or pains in your body that you can't do anything about."

"I've endured all those things," I snapped, "during the time I've spent in the human world looking for you."

Tom laughed. It was a fae laugh, hollow with fury. "Oh, so you've experienced the difference, have you? You know how many missions the queen has sent me on. I'm the only one at court who can go into the human world for her. I've been there dozens of times. You've been there, what, two weeks?"

"Four weeks," I snapped.

"Oh, well then. That makes all the difference. If it's been four weeks, you *must* know more about the human world than I do."

"I don't know more about the human world!" I shouted. "But I know more about *humans*!"

"Oh, really? And why is that?"

"Because I *am one*!"

Tom's smile fell away. For a moment, he didn't look fae at all; he looked like a fully human boy, the one who had once followed his sister into a mountain to protect her.

"I'm not like you," I said. "I never spent as much time among the fae, I never used magic as much, I never . . . *adjusted*. After only a few weeks in the human world, I already understand more about other humans than I ever did about the fae." I squeezed my eyes shut, then opened them and met Tom's gaze. "So I understand how the people of Hamelin feel, and I can't . . . I can't let them keep feeling that way. I *can't*, Tom."

He looked at the children and then at me. He passed one hand over his eyes. "All right. We'll bring them back."

"What?" Per snarled.

"What?" Anna said.

I didn't say anything, but I was also taken aback. This was exactly what I had been hoping for, and yet . . . it seemed too easy. I had no idea what I had said to change Tom's mind.

If I had really changed it.

Tom turned to the rat prince. "Have your subjects retrieve the pipe," he said, "and you have my word that once I'm done with the children, I'll give the pipe to you. You can be the one to return it to the queen."

"I don't *want* to bring the queen her pipe," Per snapped. "I want to bring her what she asked for: children."

"I'm afraid I can't allow that." Tom said it casually, but I tensed all over, prepared for another fight. "Don't worry about my mother's anger. I'll see to it that you don't suffer."

"You still owe me a favor, then," the rat prince said. "In addition to giving me the pipe. At some point in the future, I'll ask *you* for help, and you'll give me whatever I ask for."

"That seems reasonable," Tom agreed.

Which was ridiculous. None of the fae promised favors so easily. Not unless they were trying to protect something extremely important.

"Tom—" I began.

He waved me into silence. "Once we take all these children back to their town—"

"Not all of them," Anna said.

We both turned to look at her.

"I'm not going back." She turned to face Tom. "I'm going to the Realms with you."

Tom arched his eyebrows.

"You have to take me," Anna said fiercely. "You have to."

"Don't be silly," Tom said. "I don't *have* to do anything I haven't agreed to. And if you think it over carefully, I'm sure you'll realize you have no hold over me." There was something especially cruel in his slow, careless smile, something very fae. "You're human, Anna. Go where humans belong."

She clenched her fists. "I'm not like other humans."

"No?" He flicked a glance at Per. "Oh, I see. Has someone been telling you you're *special*?"

"You told me that." Anna's voice wobbled. "The first time we met, when you came to take me to the Realms. You told me that of all the children in Hamelin, you chose me."

"Did I?" Tom said. "How clever of me. I do remember that you came without a fuss. Was that why?"

"I know you meant it." Anna's voice sounded like she was scraping it along a jagged surface. "If you didn't mean it, why did you choose me?"

"Humans always want to believe they're special, and they so rarely are." My brother looked completely fae now, his mouth twisted with delight at his own cruelty.

"Do you know *why* I went to Hamelin to steal a child that first time?"

No, Tom, I thought. *Please don't tell her.*

But he wasn't looking at me. He leaned forward, focused only on Anna, his black eyes glittering. "It was because my sister wanted a friend."

I closed my eyes.

"She was lonely," Tom went on. "The queen was sending me on missions among the humans more and more often, forcing me to leave Clare alone. I would have enjoyed those missions if not for my worry about her. Humans are so *interesting*. So fun to play with. And then it occurred to me that Clare might find one interesting, too. A plaything." He hesitated, then waved a hand. "I mean playmate."

He was putting it on, acting more fae than he really was. I hated when he did that.

"Come, now," Tom drawled. "It all worked out for you, didn't it, Anna? You *liked* it in the Realms. So much so that you were desperate to come back. You have nothing to be angry at my sister about. Might as well save your energy for being angry at me."

"You *promised*." Anna sounded like she was about to cry. "You promised I would be able to stay."

"That is not entirely accurate." In the dimness, even Tom's multicolored cloak looked black, matching his hair and his eyes and the shadows dancing around his face. "Perhaps you heard only what you wanted to hear. Like humans do."

"Tom—" I began. But before I could continue, the rat prince pursed his lips and whistled.

The rats came out of the crack in a surge, as if they had been poised and waiting. The children shrieked, but the rats didn't run in their direction. They scurried around Per, between his legs, over his shoes, and then past him, into the dark crevices and cracks in the cavern walls.

The last rat to emerge carried the silver pipe clamped between its jaws, which made it move more slowly and awkwardly than the others.

Per knelt and held out one hand, and the rat deposited the pipe into his palm.

"Well done," Per murmured, and scratched the rat behind its ears. It made a purring sound, then dashed off to join the rest of the rats in the darkness.

The rat prince rose, wiped the pipe carefully on his tunic, and then held it out to Tom. "There you go," he said. "Good as new."

"Indeed it is," said a new, low, unmistakable voice.

The faerie queen detached herself from the shadows and walked across the cavern toward us. The long black train of her dress stretched across the floor, still mingled with the shadows, and her hair was as black as the cavern's darkest depths.

Tom's face went blank, the way it did when he was truly, deeply afraid.

"I'll take my pipe back now," our mother said, and held out her hand.

20

There was no disobeying a direct order from the queen. The power she wielded over the fae was absolute. They might scheme and plot behind her back, might sneak and steal and hope she didn't notice, but when she looked at you and told you her will, you bent to it. It was like obeying the earth's gravity when you fell off a cliff. There was no choice involved.

So Tom didn't disobey. But he was apparently still human enough to hesitate. Just for a second, before he walked across the cavern and placed the pipe in the queen's hand.

"Bad, bad boy," the queen murmured. She closed her fingers around the pipe. They were longer and thinner than human fingers, and had many more joints. "I should be angry at you. But how can I be upset when you've brought me all these lovely children?"

Without realizing it, I had stopped holding my breath. I immediately started again.

"I thought you'd like them." Tom bowed, pulling his cloak tightly around his body. "But this is just a sampling. I need to collect the rest before our bargain is complete."

Anna pressed her fist to her mouth, holding back muffled whimpers. The rat prince stood perfectly still, as if hoping to escape the queen's notice.

"I'm getting bored with this bargain." Our mother unfurled her wings. "Gather up the children who are here, and let's go home."

One of the youngest boys began to cry. An older boy tried desperately to keep him quiet, but his thin, terrified wails echoed through the cavern.

"What do you think, children?" the queen asked. She turned her head, her hair a sweep of shadows. "Would you like to come with me to a marvelous place where you will play games and dance all the time?"

Some of the children glanced at each other. Most of them went on staring at the queen, with her cold white face and her elongated body and her razor-sharp wings.

The queen made a face. "Oh, very well," she said, and lifted the pipe to her lips.

"No!" Anna cried.

My mother blinked. She turned her head, twisting

her neck farther than a human could have, and fixed her black eyes on Anna.

"You," she said.

I moved without thinking, stepping between my mother and my friend.

"Is there any need to take them?" I asked. My voice shook, but I made no attempt to steady it. There was no point; my mother knew I was terrified. She would have been offended if I wasn't. "You followed me to Tom. You have your pipe back. Isn't that enough?"

My mother smiled, coldly amused. "If all I wanted was my pipe, why would I have given it to my son?" She waved her hand, seemingly nonchalantly; on the wall, the shadow of her fingers came to rest on the shadow of Tom's head. "He was supposed to bring me children. We'll have to discuss his failure."

I was, for certain, the only one in the cavern aside from the queen who saw Tom's minuscule flinch.

"And yours," the queen added. I froze in terror before realizing that she wasn't talking to me. She was talking to Per.

Everyone could see Per flinch. He bowed low to the ground. "I did my part, Your Majesty."

"What does that matter? I still don't have what I want." She glanced over at me. "*You*, on the other hand. You did rather well, leading me here."

I resisted the urge to protest that I hadn't done it on purpose. The only person that would matter to was Anna, and I could explain it to her later. If I got the chance.

"You've always been your brother's weakness," the queen went on. "But you've surprised me." The shadow of her hand stroked the shadow of Tom's hair. "I believe you surprised him, too. Your brother didn't think you could handle yourself at court. But perhaps, with the proper attention and training, you could be quite useful."

"Only if she wanted to be." Tom's voice cracked; even the humans could hear his terror now. "But she doesn't, and she won't."

"Are you sure? Look how well she managed today. All she needed was the right motivation." The queen pursed her lips, which made her cheekbones as sharp as her wings. "You're underestimating your sister. I'm quite pleased with her. In fact, I'm not sure I need you anymore."

"Then may I have a reward?" I blurted out.

I didn't realize I was going to say it until I did. My mother stared at me in astonishment. I had never asked her for anything. I had never tried to protect Tom before. It had always been him protecting me.

Under the ice-cold weight of my mother's stare, I remembered why.

Her wings spread wide, casting the cavern into shadow. "Of course. What do you want?"

My mind went blank. I hadn't actually expected her to agree; I had just been trying to distract her, the way Tom did whenever she focused on *me*.

"I," I said, "I want—"

Some years ago, a dryad had asked the queen for a favor, and the queen had turned her into stone as punishment. The dryad had pleaded for mercy as grayness crept up her legs, but it had been too late. Once you asked, you couldn't take it back.

"I want to bring these children back to Hamelin," I said.

The queen drew herself up, her shadow stretching along the ceiling, and fixed her black gaze on me.

Another time, an elf had asked to sew her a new gown. She had deemed that an impertinence and buried him alive. We had all watched as the ground sucked him in, slowly and inexorably, while he thrashed and apologized and begged.

From the corner of my eye, I saw Tom step forward, his jaw taut.

"I suggest," my mother said, "that you choose a different reward."

I glanced sideways at my brother. He shook his head, very slightly, from side to side.

I swallowed hard. My mother had phrased it as a suggestion, because even the queen would never break a promise. She *couldn't* order me to take it back, not after she had already agreed to give me a reward.

Tom shook his head again, more violently. Telling me what I needed to do to stay safe.

"This is the reward I want," I said. My heart felt like it was lunging out of my throat, but my voice was steadier than it had been before. "I want to give the children back to their parents. Alive."

The queen examined me as if I was a particularly interesting spiderweb she hadn't previously noticed. Pretty and unexpected, but easily torn apart.

"Very well," she said. "You may take them back."

"She can't," Tom said. "She needs the pipe to get them across the border."

The queen looked at him, and the expression on her face would have made anyone else stagger back. But Tom stood his ground.

"I suppose you're right," the queen said finally. She turned toward me, her hair sweeping again in an arc that momentarily blocked the light from the stalactite chandeliers.

I flinched. It took me a moment to realize that she was holding the pipe out to me.

"Go on," she said. "Take it. But you must promise that you will give it back."

Never make promises to the queen. It wasn't just Tom who

had told me that; all the fae knew it. Promises in general were dangerous. The fae might lie and cheat and steal as easily as they breathed, but promises and bargains were sacred.

I knew I should refuse. But it had taken everything I had to defy my mother once, and I couldn't do it again. I nodded.

My hand shook so hard it took me several tries to close my fingers around the pipe. Once I did, though, a surge of power went straight through me and steadied me. The pipe felt almost weightless, as if it was made of something far lighter than silver. It tingled against my skin, calm and bright and wild. I drew it to my side.

"Good," my mother said, and smiled at me. No— smiled *back* at me. I hadn't realized until then that I was smiling. I glanced down at the pipe gleaming in my hand. "When you bring it back, I'll teach you to play it properly."

It was the first time she had ever offered to teach me anything. I knew she would forget, but warmth still rushed through me, from the new steadiness in my feet to the tingling in my fingertips. I nodded.

"Now go save your children," my mother said. "As for the rest of you . . ."

Without looking away from me, she waved a hand sideways.

Fear flashed across Per's face. The stones beneath his feet bulged and lengthened, stalagmites bursting from the ground and curving around him. Before he had time to react—not that there was anything he could have done—he was inside a cage, thin lines of rock twining up around him and extending toward the ceiling.

Anna screamed, and I whirled. She was enclosed in a separate stalagmite cage, her cane lying on the ground outside the bars. She wrapped her arms around herself and began to sob.

"No!" I said, and Tom shot me a sharp look. But my mother was still smiling at me, and I couldn't stop myself. "Don't kill them. Please."

"Who said anything about killing them? I'm just going to leave them here for a while." The queen flowed forward—as if her shadow was pulling her along, rather than the other way around—and reached a slim hand between the bars to stroke Anna's cheek. The stalagmites curved apart to let her hand through. Anna stood frozen with terror. The queen smiled at her with a terrible gentleness. She pulled her hand out, and the stone bars straightened.

Then she turned to me, and my heart contracted into a tiny knot.

"Unless," she said, "you decide to complete your

brother's bargain. If the two of you bring the children to me, instead of bringing them home, I'll let your friend go."

I couldn't think. I could barely breathe. I felt myself nod.

"Excellent." She reached out, and for a moment I thought she was going to touch me, too. My entire body tightened in anticipation. But all I felt was a cool waft of air against my skin. "Please do make sure to bring them to me alive. Humans are entirely useless once they're dead."

Then she vanished, leaving only the sound of her laughter echoing among the rocks.

21

"Well," Tom said. "That went well."

"Tom." My throat was so tight I could barely get his name out. "Don't."

"Don't what?" he asked innocently.

"Don't act all uncaring and sardonic and . . . and . . . *fae*. Not now." I clenched the pipe so tightly my knuckles hurt. The children were silent for once—even the two redheads, who stared at me with wide, frightened eyes. My heart twisted. "I can't do it. I can't give them to her."

Tom sighed. "So don't. Bring them to Hamelin."

"I can't leave Anna in a cage!"

"That doesn't seem to leave you with a lot of options."

"You don't understand! She's not like us. She can't—"

A loud thud sounded from behind me. I whirled just in time to see Anna kick the stalagmites around her.

They broke in a series of cracks and crumbled in several large pieces to the cavern floor, along with a shower of dust. Then she stepped right over them.

"Stalagmites are actually pretty fragile," she explained, crossing the floor to us. "They're hollow." She stopped to brush dust off her skirt, then felt our gazes on her and looked up. "What?"

It had been a long time since I'd seen Tom look shocked. I might have enjoyed it more if not for the fact that my expression was probably similar to his.

Anna's brow furrowed. She looked over at Per, who was still in his own cage, the stalagmites so close around him that he could barely move. "It doesn't take much. Just a couple of kicks—"

"But the queen put me here," Per said.

"So? She's not here anymore. Just break yourself out."

He stared at her as if she was speaking a foreign language. Which she was, to anyone who had grown up in the Realms. Everybody had to obey the queen. Her power over the fae was absolute.

"He can't break himself out," I said. "It would be disobeying the queen. That's not possible for the fae."

"Right." Anna shook her cane to get the rock dust off it. "Well, it's possible for me. So I'll break you out."

Tom leaned back on his heels, looking half horrified and half amused. "If you kick the stalagmites in from the outside, you'll be propelling them right at him. And they look pretty sharp to me."

Anna frowned. "Then what do we do?"

"We leave him here," Tom said cheerfully. "Which gives us the bonus of not having to worry that he'll attack us again." He looked at us. "Any objections?"

Anna bit her lip and looked at Per, then at me. I folded my arms across my chest and shook my head.

"Excellent!" Tom said. "Let's be on our way."

Per cleared his throat. "So. About that favor you owe me . . ."

Tom made a face. "I don't suppose you're going to ask for cake? I've been told recently that I summon up *very* good cake."

Per didn't bother to respond.

"Fine." Tom tapped a finger against his chin, considering the problem. "I suppose I could use the pipe to disintegrate the stalagmites around you. The trouble is, I can't disobey the queen any more than you can."

"You're human," Per grated out. "You can do what you want."

"Can I?" Tom considered it. "I'm not sure I can. The more magic I use, the more fae I become. And I've been using a *lot* of magic lately."

Far above, something rumbled. A few of the children began to cry again.

"I'll do it," I said.

Tom's head snapped around. I held up the pipe. "Is it the same tune you used to crumble the rocks earlier? I'm pretty sure I remember it." I put the pipe to my lips and blew.

A long, hoarse squeak came out the other end. I flushed. "Sorry. It's been a while since I played a musical instrument."

Tom narrowed his eyes. I wondered if he was remembering the last time: at a dance where an elven princess had let us borrow her magic flute. Tom had taught me to play it. It hadn't taken long; magical instruments generally played themselves, once you got them started.

I tried the pipe again. This time, a respectable—if thin—sound came out.

"Clare," Tom said. "It's not that easy. I don't think—"

The sound strengthened, without my doing much to make it happen. I felt the power in the pipe waken, and my hands flew over the holes. The tune I remembered burst from the pipe, soaring into a long, lively trill.

The stalagmites around Per crumbled into dust. So did all the stalagmites on the cavern floor, including the column Tom had been sitting on.

I grinned triumphantly and lowered the pipe. For a moment, I didn't understand why I was still hearing music. Then I realized that I hadn't lowered the pipe at all; my mind had decided to stop playing, but my hands hadn't. My fingers danced along the holes and the tune soared. Stalactites began to break from the ceiling and shatter on the ground.

I tried to curl one hand into a fist, pinkie out, to let Tom know I wasn't doing this on purpose. But I couldn't control my hands enough to make the signal, and I couldn't stop blowing into the pipe long enough to call him.

"Clare!" Anna screamed, and Tom dashed forward and pulled me backward. A huge, triangular stone plummeted into the space where I had been standing. It shattered into dozens of shards, and a sharp pain burned along my arm. I barely had time to register the gush of blood before the magic running through me sealed the wound up. I didn't even stop playing. I *couldn't* stop playing.

Several stalactites fell yards away from me, smashing to the ground in clouds of dust.

"Children!" Anna shouted. "With me, into the tunnel! Quick!"

Per dashed across the cavern in rat form, narrowly avoiding a shower of fist-sized rocks. Another stalactite plummeted toward me, and I used the pipe's magic to fling it sideways, where it exploded harmlessly against a ledge. I was vaguely aware of panic rising in me, but

I could barely spare enough attention to notice it. All I could feel was the magic and the music twining together, spilling from my breath into the pipe. People were screaming, calling my name, but they were also drowned out by the music. There was nothing but music, and I was never going to stop playing the pipe, never—

"Clare." I hadn't realized Tom was next to me until I heard his voice right in my ear. A second later, I realized that his hand was around my upper arm. "Give it to me."

My fingers tightened around the pipe. But I turned and looked into my brother's eyes, dark and deep and warm, and unexpected relief flowed through me. I let the magic go.

Stones continued to fall around us, shattering when they hit the ground. Tom pulled me in tight and held up one hand. I felt his magic surge as the stones bounced off the air above our heads.

He peeled my fingers off the pipe. I started to fight him, but he said, "Clare," and I forced myself to stop just long enough for him to pull the pipe free.

The mouthpiece slipped from my lips, and all at once I could breathe again. Tom tucked the pipe into a pocket of his cloak. I met his eyes.

"Thank you," I whispered. My voice came out hoarse.

He nodded. "Now," he said, "let's get out of here."

Rocks slid down the walls and rolled across the ground, and my brother and I ran together through a cloud of dust and pebbles. By the time we reached the safety of the tunnel, my eyes were burning from the dust and I was coughing so hard my chest hurt. As I leaned across a wall to recover, an avalanche of rocks cascaded across the mouth of the tunnel, sealing us off from the cavernous ballroom and plunging us into darkness.

Tom and Per pulled up glow lights simultaneously, and we stood there looking at each other in the white light. Most of the children were squeezing their eyes shut against the dust, and Anna had both her hands over her face. I used a flick of magic to clear the air around my mouth and nose.

"Well," Per said, "on the plus side, that tune *was* very pretty."

The ceiling rumbled, and I realized that the tunnel might not be safe after all. I pushed myself upright. "How do we get out of here?"

"Follow me." Tom turned.

"Wait," Anna said, uncovering her eyes. I used another smidge of magic to keep the dust away from her face. "There's a dragon at the end of this tunnel."

"It was sleeping," I added quickly.

Anna let out a choked laugh. "I think we might have woken it up."

"From that?" Per glanced at the jumble of boulders jammed against the tunnel entrance and snorted. "I doubt it. Dragons sleep almost as deeply as teenagers."

"It's all right," Tom said. "I know another way. There's a turnoff you probably didn't see. It will take us on a more direct route to the portal."

"Us?" Anna repeated.

"I'm coming too, of course." He glanced at me and grinned. "I'm obviously needed to keep this one out of trouble."

Which made me feel warm and prickly at the same time. I'd spent weeks in the human world, and I had managed just fine. I didn't need protection there, not like I did in the Realms.

But the prickles faded almost immediately when Tom walked over to stand next to me. He was tall and solid, a familiar protective presence. My muscles relaxed one by one. He put a hand on my shoulder, and for the first time in weeks, I felt safe.

That feeling lasted for less than a second, until Per said, "I'm coming too."

"Fair enough," Tom agreed. "Once we're done with the children, I'll give you the pipe. You can return it to my mother. That way you'll fulfill my sister's promise to her and also earn her favor."

"What?" Anna said. "He can't come with us!"

Tom raised his eyebrows. "Why ever not?"

"Because . . . because . . . ," Anna spluttered, then whirled to me. "How can you trust him after he attacked us?"

"I didn't trust him before he attacked us, either," I pointed out.

"We don't have time to argue," Tom said. As if to emphasize his point, there was a cracking sound from above, and a small avalanche of rocks slid down one of the tunnel walls.

Anna looked up apprehensively. I narrowed my eyes at my brother. There was no *as if* about it; he had done that on purpose.

He blinked at me innocently. "I think," he said, "that we should get moving. Let's bring these children back to Hamelin."

My whole body was gripped by a sudden chill. My brother was at his most dangerous when he seemed innocent.

"Tom," I said, but he turned and sauntered away. Anna rushed to catch up to him, talking urgently—I made out the words *children* and *Realms*—and before I could protest, the children streamed after them.

I stood as still as if I had turned into one of the cave's pillars, suddenly realizing what I had done. Too late, too late.

I had underestimated my brother's ruthlessness, and I had no excuse for it; I had grown up with him in the Realms, where affection and coldness, joy and fear, swirled in ever-changing currents. I had watched him gain acceptance in the fae court, learn to play their games, make himself useful to the queen. I had seen him become coldly ambitious like the rest of them.

I should have known he wasn't giving up.

I didn't know why he was bringing the children back to Hamelin first. He had them all here, including Anna—he could have fulfilled his bargain then and there. No one could have stopped him, certainly not me.

Maybe he just didn't want to fight with me.

I wrapped my arms around my body. I didn't understand exactly what my brother was doing, but I was sure, bone-deep, that he hadn't given up. I shouldn't have let myself believe, even for a second, that he was bringing the children back to Hamelin to save them.

He was bringing them back so he could try again.

22

"I believe I know," Per said, "why the queen wasn't sure we could keep them alive. But even if I kill just a few of the children, we'll still have brought *most* of them back alive."

"No," I said.

"Just the redheaded boy, then. I'm sure his parents won't miss *him*."

The redheaded boy chose that moment to kick a rock across the path. It bounced off a stalagmite and hit a little girl's leg. She burst into tears.

I gritted my teeth. Anna quickly went to the crying girl. She picked her up and carried her while the girl wailed and thrashed and kicked.

I unclenched my jaw. In the narrow passageway, everything the children did sounded about three times louder than it was. "His mother does miss him. We're not killing *any* of the children."

"What if we just *lose* a couple, then?" Per said. "We could always come back for them later."

"*Tom,*" I appealed to my brother.

But Tom didn't seem to hear me. He was walking slightly ahead, clenching the pipe so tightly that if it hadn't been a magical object, he might have broken it. His brief conversation with Anna had left him in a foul mood. (Anna didn't look too happy, either.) Even though I kept hurrying to catch up to Tom, he still hadn't said another word to me.

Which was probably for the best, because I couldn't think of anything to say to him.

I tried to imagine an argument, or a plea, that would get him to abandon his bargain with our mother. But I had fooled myself long enough; I couldn't do it anymore. I couldn't make myself believe that anything I said would make a difference.

I have to try, I thought. I couldn't give up, not on the children and not on my brother. But every time we stopped and I had an opportunity to talk to him again, I glanced at his thin, angular, familiar face and my throat closed up.

We had to stop a lot, to urge some children to walk faster and to keep others from running on ahead. Most often, though, we stopped to bring them into side tunnels so they could relieve themselves. Anna, who knew more than the rest of us about children, had told them to relieve themselves soon after we started off. They had all sworn they didn't have to. But we had already stopped for ten privy breaks. And that wasn't counting the boy who refused to go but kept whining that his stomach hurt, which was clearly because he wouldn't go. And when they didn't need to go, they were hungry and thirsty, so Tom kept summoning up more cakes (which clearly wasn't helping with the stomachaches, though I had to admit they were delicious) and directing water from underground streams to sluice over the rocks so we could drink from them.

The majority of our stops were for the two redheads. Their names were Alf and Binnie. Learning their names had involved three separate fights: one over Alf pronouncing Binnie's name wrong, one over Binnie claiming Alf had lied about his age (I still didn't know which of them was telling the truth, and I didn't care), and one over Binnie saying she wished Alf *wasn't* her brother, which enraged Alf so much that he shoved her into a stalagmite, which made her scream as if she was being murdered.

"You're not even *bleeding*," Alf said scornfully, as if that was the only question at hand.

She kicked him.

Behind me, a child said, "I have to go potty."

"*Tom,*" I said. "Can you *play the pipe,* please?"

Tom looked at me over his shoulder. "What, and 'take away their free will'?"

"Yes," I said. "I've thought it over, and I'm okay with that now."

He shook his head. "If I play the pipe, the queen will know that I'm the one who has it. I don't think that would be a good idea. Not while we're still so deep within the Realms."

"Ew!" a girl screeched, and a little ashamed voice said, "I couldn't hold it in."

"You stink!"

"No, *you* stink!"

"I think it would be worth the risk," I said. "Could her punishment really be any worse than this?"

Tom looked down at the pipe, clearly tempted. But he didn't lift it. "Back in the cavern, when I played a calming spell, it didn't work on those two."

He didn't have to specify which two. Alf was pulling Binnie's hair, and Binnie was trying to bite him.

I sighed. "Let's just get them all back to Hamelin as soon as possible. I'm sure their parents know how to deal with them."

"Are you?" Tom arched an eyebrow. "Their parents didn't do a great job of holding on to them the first time I came."

My stomach clenched. Time to try again. "But they won't have to protect them from *you* this time," I said. "Will they?"

Tom looked away.

Which gave me hope. None of the other fae would have been ashamed enough to look away. "Tom, do you remember when—"

"I BANGED MY TOE!" a boy wailed.

"I'm hungry!" a girl cried from the back of the line. "We're all hungry!"

"You've had cake," Tom said defensively. "Lots of cake. And pies."

"My feet hurt!" the boy behind us said.

Alf skipped up next to us, apparently recovered from his fight with Binnie. "Can I play the pipe?"

"No," Tom said shortly.

"Can I hold it?"

"No."

"Can I see it?"

Tom ground his teeth together. "You're looking at it right now!"

"Can I look at it more closely?"

"No!"

"Can I—"

"We're here!" Tom announced, coming to a stop.

That did not make a difference to the boy with the

stubbed toe, who went on wailing. But the other children went suddenly quiet. They looked around at the walls, which were now illuminated by the two glow lights.

"We are?" Anna said. "Here—where?"

Tom turned and put his hand on a stretch of relatively smooth wall. "Once I start playing the pipe, this portal will open and you can all walk through."

"That sounds scary," Alf said. "I don't want to walk through that."

"I'll do it." Another boy pushed past him. "*I'm* not scared."

"You should be," Alf said. "What if it turns *back* to stone while you're walking through and you get stuck inside it?"

Binnie burst into tears. Two other children followed suit.

"It won't!" Tom said. "It will be just like when we went through the first time. Wasn't that fun?"

"No!" a boy wailed.

"Yes, it was! You all *laughed*!"

"We didn't," a girl said. "We were crying."

"I was *right there*—" Tom gave up. He shook his head and lifted the pipe to his lips.

The piercing notes danced across the wall. The rocks shimmered with colors—colors I could see, and colors I could sense but not see—and then there was an opening in the wall, and beyond it we could see trees and bushes and a vast blue sky.

I stepped prudently out of the way. Per was not quite as fast, and he got knocked aside as the children streamed forward, pushing and shoving each other.

"Ouch!"

"Me *first!*"

"You HIT me!"

"I'll hit you again if you don't *move!*"

Per scrambled to my side and stood with his back pressed against the wall. Anna came to join us. We watched the children run down the path.

"STOP EATING ALL THE BERRIES!"

"You shouldn't eat those berries! They could be poisonous!"

"Don't be a dolt, I know what poisonous berries look like!"

"Don't call me a dolt!"

"Don't tell me what to do!"

"I could close up the portal," Tom suggested, "and we could stay here. I'm sure they'll find their way home on their own."

"Yes!" I said instantly. "That's an excellent idea."

Tom chuckled, as if we were in on the same joke.

"I'm serious," I said. "Tom—"

A whiff of magic from Per interrupted me. I flinched,

but he was merely shifting. Instead of a blond boy, a giant rat crouched on the ground next to us.

Anna shrieked and stepped away from him.

Per shimmered back into a boy and looked at her mournfully. "I'm still the same person, you know. No matter what shape I'm in."

"Why did you change?" Anna demanded.

"Because I'm coming with you." She continued to stare at him, and he sighed. "I'm bound by the Pact. I can't cross the border in human form. Outside the Realms, I can only be a rat."

Anna turned to me. "Is that true? He won't be able to take his true form on the other side of the portal?"

"That *is* his true form," I said. "He is literally a rat."

Per gave me a sad, hurt look. Then, when Anna wasn't watching, he smirked and wiggled his cheeks as if they had whiskers.

By the time Anna turned back to him, his expression was doleful again. "I hope," he said earnestly, "that you won't treat me differently just because I'm forced to take on this shape."

"*I* definitely won't treat you differently," I said.

He shifted back into a rat and lashed his tail against my leg. Then he scurried out of the tunnel and disappeared into the bushes.

I rubbed my stinging calf. "I don't like this," I said. "Why do we need him along?"

"We don't," Tom said. "He probably wants to make sure I survive to grant him his favor."

"But you don't owe him a favor anymore. I got him out of the cage. . . ." I trailed off. I had forgotten to specify, before I freed Per, that it was in payment of Tom's favor. *Stupid, stupid.* I took a deep breath. "Do you know what he's going to ask of you when he calls the favor in?"

"No idea."

"Don't you think you should worry about that?"

"Of course," Tom said. "I plan to worry about it constantly." He gestured toward the portal. "But first things first. After you."

———◆———

Once we left the caves, we caught up to the children easily. Luckily, we had emerged in the early morning, so we would reach Hamelin before nightfall.

Or so I thought. After a dozen more privy breaks and twenty stops for injuries and fights, I wasn't as sure. The sun was dipping toward the horizon by the time we saw the town's brown rooftops up ahead.

That sight rejuvenated the children. Even the ones who had been walking at approximately the speed of an exhausted turtle now broke into a run, screaming with excitement.

Two of them immediately tripped and fell. One got up and began running again; the other curled up on the ground wailing. Anna strode forward, her cane tapping swiftly, and knelt next to him, leaving me and Tom alone.

Finally.

I stopped walking and turned to my brother. He watched the children with a bemused expression. "I guess they're eager to get home?" he said.

"Of course they are," I said. "Did you think they wouldn't be?"

Tom shrugged. "They seemed happy in the caves. Playing games, eating cake...."

I folded my arms across my chest. "Did you think about their parents?"

"I don't think their parents gave them enough cake."

"I mean," I said, "didn't you think they would miss their parents? Or that their parents would care that they were gone?"

In my imagination I heard a breathy twitter, the fae laughing at me for my human foolishness.

But Tom never laughed at me, not for any of the clumsy human things I said or did. He looked at me with interest. "*Did* they care?"

"Yes, Tom. They did."

"But they're human. Can't they just have more children?" He considered. "I suppose some of them are too old."

"That's not—" My throat tightened. It had realized my next question before I did. "Wouldn't you miss *me*, if someone took me far away?"

Tom gave me a sharper look than I had expected. "Not if I knew you were safe and happy."

"I would miss you," I said. "I *did* miss you."

His shoulders twitched. "You would forget, in time. Eventually I would be just a memory."

"That's not how it works. The parents will grieve forever if you take their children away. I know it doesn't make sense, but it's true."

Tom's face was blank. I wasn't making any headway. And I was running out of time.

"I don't want you to do this," I said. "If you do, I'll never forgive you."

Tom's eyes narrowed. "*Forgive* me? If not for you, none of this would be happening."

His words were like a blow—worse than a blow. He had never before blamed me for leading him into the Realms, back when I had been barely more than a baby. He had never once mentioned it.

But obviously, he had never forgotten it.

"Mama!" a girl cried, and I whirled, grateful for an excuse to look away from Tom.

The road was no longer empty. The residents of Hamelin were streaming toward us, racing from the town to meet their children.

The two waves met and merged. Children were swung up into the air, held tightly, and covered with kisses. Everyone was crying, the parents sobbing louder than their children.

No. Not everyone.

I blinked, not understanding what I was seeing. There were children *in* the group coming from Hamelin. They weren't crying; they were excited, weaving through the mass of adults, greeting their friends with grins and questions. A few of the adults chased after them, pulling them back.

I stared at these children I had never seen before: clean, bright-cheeked, happy. I watched them for several seconds without comprehending. Then I turned and saw the covered wagon Anna and I had come across in the field. It was unhitched from the horses and set at a tilt near the town's entrance.

We're bringing them back to Hamelin, the red-haired man had said. *Them.* The children in the wagon.

Children who had been hidden away from the Pied Piper when he came to town.

My breath was having trouble leaving my body. It formed a heavy, tangled knot in my chest.

Some of the children got left behind. I had assumed Tom was talking about Anna. But he had spoken in the plural; he had been talking about *these* children.

And there was only one possible reason why these children had been spared. Why the mayor would have had some children hidden before Tom came to steal the rest.

He had known Tom was coming. And he had known he was coming for the children.

I didn't ask them for money, Tom had told me. Of course he hadn't. That had been a lie the mayor told his people. The deal Tom had made with the mayor had been a lot more straightforward. Tom had demanded the town's children in exchange for getting rid of the rats.

And the mayor had agreed.

They'll be safer in the Realms, Tom had said. I should have listened.

Because the children hadn't been stolen by my brother. They had been *traded* to him. Sold.

And I had just brought them back to the person who had sold them.

23

"Tom," I said.

My brother looked down at me. His face was all angles, his eyes piercing beneath slashes of black eyebrows. Here in the human world, he looked more fae than ever, a sharp outline against the dull, mundane air.

"Heartwarming reunion," he said, "isn't it?"

My heart wasn't the slightest bit warmed. "The mayor never offered you money," I said, "did he?"

Tom's brow furrowed in puzzlement. "What would I do with money?"

Of course he hadn't asked for money. It wasn't for gold that my mother had given Tom her pipe and sent him into the human world. It wasn't for gold that Tom had asked for the rat prince's help.

It wasn't gold that the mayor had offered him.

The mayor had given him the town's *children*.

But not all the town's children. And that was why Tom hadn't brought them to the queen. There was no point in giving her only part of what she had bargained for.

Someone yanked my skirt so hard I heard the flimsy material rip. I looked down. Binnie was clinging to me, her round face covered with tears. Alf stood behind her with his arms crossed over his chest.

I looked around. Every other child was in the arms of an adult, but I didn't see the red-haired woman who had given me the picture.

"We can't find our mama!" Binnie sobbed. "Something happened to her!"

I remembered the desperation on their mother's face, and my heart sank. Something *must* have happened to her or she would be here.

"The other children said she's in prison," Alf said. His lower lip wobbled.

So their mother was a criminal. That made sense. "I, um—"

Binnie let out a wail and held her arms up to me. Before I knew what I was doing, I bent and scooped her up, holding her the way the other children were being held. She buried her face in my shoulder and wrapped her spindly arms around my neck.

"Thank you!" a voice boomed through the crowd. "Thank you for bringing back our children!"

Mayor Herman strode through the suddenly silent townspeople, radiating joy and triumph. Anna walked next to him, her hand in his, her head bowed.

"We placed our hope in you," the mayor pronounced, "and you did not disappoint us." He beamed at me, so sincerely that a part of me wanted to smile back. "You have our undying gratitude!"

The crowd broke into cheers.

"No!" I said. "That's not what happened."

Nobody heard me over the sounds of merriment. The mayor stood in the center of the crowd, beaming, and the joy swelled around him, an unstoppable wave.

"Stop." I raised my voice. "You're still in danger!"

The people nearest to me turned, their joy fading into resentful wariness.

"There is always danger," Mayor Herman declared. "But we have our children back, and together, we can face whatever comes." He lifted both his hands over his head. "I declare tomorrow a day of festivities!"

Everyone in the crowd burst into cheers. Except for Binnie, who was wiping her nose on my shirt, and Alf, whose stony expression hadn't changed. And Anna, who kept staring at the ground.

"Wait," I said, but my voice was low and small. Nobody so much as glanced my way.

I grabbed the arm of the woman next to me. "Listen to me. Please!"

The woman looked at me, and I saw that she had a child in her arms—a plump boy with red cheeks who had not been with us in the caves. I dropped her arm and stepped back, and she narrowed her eyes at me.

Of course. Some of these people, the one whose children had been hidden . . . they had known, too.

The mayor hadn't used magic on them, the way Tom had with the children. They'd had a choice. They had gone along with his plan because they wanted to.

How many of them were in this crowd? I looked around the square, trying to figure it out. It was a mass of humans, some happy to have their children back, some who had always had their children. I had no idea who I could trust, and I was pretty sure none of them would be receptive to what I had to say.

Which meant it couldn't come from me. But if the mayor's own daughter told them . . .

"Anna!" I called, and she looked at me, and that was when my brain finally caught up with the most devastating realization of all.

Anna, too, had known.

She was the mayor's daughter. He had sent her to safety with the others. *That* was the real reason she hadn't followed Tom along with the other children. That was why her father had been shocked when she showed up in his office. And that was why she hadn't wanted me to know what the wagon in the field held.

Because she had known it held children. The children of her father's friends, hidden in safety while the other children were traded away.

I stood there, unable to speak, unable to even breathe, while the mayor turned to Tom. "We have learned our lesson. We will, of course, pay you your thousand guilders. We just need a little time to get it."

"I'm happy to wait." Tom grinned, his teeth flashing white. "I've never been to a human festival."

"You will be our guest of honor!" the mayor declared.

"NO!" Alf shouted. "This isn't right! Where's our mother?"

I looked down at him. My heart twisted at the expression on his face, but behind that came a realization: there was at least *one* person in this town who would listen to me.

I looked at the mayor. "Every parent in Hamelin should be reunited with their children," I said, trying to copy his dramatic, ringing tone. It didn't really work.

The mayor's face tightened. "Their mother was making wild, irresponsible accusations and causing panic. Regrettably, she had to be imprisoned."

I stepped toward him. Or I tried to. Alf grabbed my skirt and pulled me back, which made me trip and stumble. In the process, I almost dropped Binnie, who grabbed me around the neck with a shriek.

"Don't go to him!" Alf shouted. "He's bad and EVIL!"

"*I know,*" I tried to hiss. But Binnie's grip was choking me, and I was starting to see spots. With a wrench, I pulled her arms away from my neck and dumped her on the ground. She stared at me, stunned, then began to sob as if I had deposited her on a bed of sharp nails.

I turned around. Mayor Herman looked exactly how I felt, impatient and annoyed.

Which maybe meant I should try *not* to feel that way. Given the mayor's evilness.

I bent down and picked Binnie up again, holding her under the arms so she couldn't grab my neck. I smiled at her as kindly as I could.

She kicked me in the stomach.

I held her farther away. "No matter what their mother has done," I said, through gritted teeth, "I'm sure she wants to see her children. And to *take care of them.*"

Binnie was still wailing and kicking, but Alf had gone silent. The mayor looked from him to Binnie to me. Then he glanced at the townspeople, who had stopped cheering and were listening intently.

"Of course," he said. He lifted one hand. "I hereby issue a one-day pardon for all crimes so everyone can join in the celebration of our children's return!"

Screams of joy. The mayor certainly knew how to work a crowd.

And I, very obviously, did not.

Anna pulled her hand free of her father's grip. "I'll take you to the prison," she offered, tilting her head so her hair half covered her face.

"No," the mayor said. "You're coming with me." He gestured at his henchmen. "One of you, lead them to the prison."

The bearded henchman—the one who had been so eager to hit me in the mayor's office—stepped up. He had trimmed his beard a bit since the last time I saw him, which gave me a better look at his face. Judging by his expression, his feelings on the whole hitting-me issue hadn't changed.

But this time I wasn't facing him alone. I smiled at Mayor Herman, showing all my teeth.

"Anna will take me," I said. "Don't you think that's best, Tom?"

Tom twirled the pipe in his hand. "Definitely," he said. "We still have so much to talk about."

I heard the mayor's teeth grind together. Anna

turned to her father and held her hand out, her expression much the same as it had been when she maneuvered him into letting her go with me that first time.

Mayor Herman scowled, but he detached a key from his belt and dropped it into his daughter's palm.

"Be careful," he said. "Don't trust either of them."

Anna turned away from him. "Let's go," she said to me.

Alf immediately darted down the road ahead of us. Apparently, he knew exactly where the prison was located.

We followed Alf through the gray, narrow streets. I matched my step with Tom's, who had fallen in on my other side. I heard Anna draw in her breath once or twice, as if she was about to say something. But it wasn't until Alf came to a stop—in front of a rather ordinary-looking cottage with iron bars across its windows—that she broke her silence. "I'm sorry, Clare."

I didn't look at her. I was afraid that if I did, I would start crying, and I wasn't going to cry in front of Tom. Not over a *human*.

"I know I should have told you," Anna said miserably. "I wanted to. I wanted to tell you everything. But I just . . . I was too ashamed."

"Why?" Tom said.

She hunched her shoulders. "You wouldn't understand."

She was right; he wouldn't. The fae did not feel shame. Not for anything they did, and certainly not for something someone else had done.

But *I* understood. I remembered the tremor that had gone through me when I heard about what Tom had done to the children of Hamelin, and the guilt that had driven me to this town to see if I could undo it.

I wasn't used to understanding things that Tom didn't. It made my gut twist.

Anna turned to face me. "I never meant for any of this to happen. I didn't want anyone to get hurt. I was just so unhappy, and I couldn't think about anyone but myself." She bit her lip. "I mean . . . I could have. But I didn't. I wish I could take it back."

"Do you?" Tom said. He sounded vastly amused, probably at the very idea of someone apologizing for thinking only of themselves.

I kicked him in the leg, then dodged back before he could swat me.

"Yes," Anna said. "Yes, of course I do! If I'd known how things would turn out, I'd do everything differently."

"This is one of the interesting contrasts," Tom said to me, "between the Realms and the human world.

The fae are good at lying. But humans don't even know when they're lying."

His tone was calm and careful—the voice he used to explain things to me, to lecture me on how to survive. Irritation prickled all over my skin, and I turned my back on him.

"It's all right," I said to Anna. "I did the same thing when I asked Tom to bring me a friend."

Anna sighed. "Thank you, but it's not the same at all. You don't understand."

"No," Tom murmured, "I'd say she doesn't."

"Fine," I snapped. I'd just about had it with my brother. "Why don't you assume I don't understand anything, and go ahead and explain it to me. Be sure to speak slowly and use really simple words."

Tom lifted a scornful eyebrow—not at me, but at Anna. "Go ahead," he said to her.

"Not her. *You.*" I stepped toward him. "How can I get you to stop this?"

"You can't," he said. "Let it go, Clare. I know what I'm doing."

"But *I* don't know what you're doing!"

"You don't need to know."

I clenched my fists so hard that one of my knuckles cracked. "Tell me what the bargain was for," I said. "What did Mother offer you, to make you agree to do this? It must be something important. But maybe there's another way to get it. I can help you, we can—just tell me what you asked her for."

He shook his head.

Tom had never refused to tell me anything before. He'd answered every question I had about the Realms and the court and his activities in the human world, even when the answers were horrifying and unsuitable for little girls. He'd always said I needed to know the truth if I was to protect myself.

Did he no longer care about keeping me safe? Or was there some other reason he didn't want me to know? Was he afraid I would use it against him?

Was he right?

"Tom," I said. But my voice cracked and I couldn't go on.

I thought I saw his face soften. But when he spoke, his voice was cool and casual. "You have to trust me, little sister. I've got this handled. And right now we have a festival to look forward to."

He pulled his cloak around himself very dramatically. Under any other circumstances, I would have rolled my eyes.

"Smile, Clare," he said. "Everything is going exactly the way I want it to."

24

I didn't smile. Tom's grin dropped away as he looked down at me, and I wondered what he saw on my face.

"Listen to me," I pleaded. My voice quavered, on the edge of tears, and I hated that he heard it and that his expression didn't change. "Tom—"

"Anna!" the mayor roared.

We all whirled. Mayor Herman was striding up the street toward us, his face red. His bearded henchman was right behind him.

Anna fumbled with the key and dropped it into my hand. "I had better go. Let the prisoners out before he changes his mind."

I hesitated. The mayor's boots hit the cobblestones more loudly than seemed necessary. "What is he going to do to you?"

"I'll be fine," Anna said. "He won't hurt *me*. I'll find you later." She turned and walked down the street toward her father. She walked more quickly now that she was on familiar streets, not bothering to use her cane.

"This is taking A MILLION YEARS!" Alf shouted. He lunged forward, grabbed the key out of my hand, and dashed up the few stairs to the front door.

Tom and I strode after him. We reached the threshold just as Alf turned the key and pulled the door open.

A handful of rough-looking men sat in a large, dimly lit room. They turned and stared at us hard-eyed, except for one man who lay on a straw pallet watching the ceiling.

The red-haired woman from the square was not among the prisoners.

I stepped up next to Tom and cleared my throat. "The children are back!"

The prisoners didn't move.

"The mayor," Tom announced, "is freeing you all from prison so you can celebrate."

He pulled me to the side as the men stampeded through the door. The floor shook beneath us, and I pressed my back against the doorpost, turning my face to the side. Clearly, there were no baths in prison.

The man on the pallet still lay there. I coughed, which helped get the smell out of my throat, but got no reaction from him. "Um, we said—"

"I heard," he said in a slurred voice. "I'm just going to stay here." He turned over and closed his eyes.

Then the door at the end of the room opened, and the red-haired woman from the square stepped out. She was no longer wearing a kerchief, and her hair hung in dirty tangles over her face. She stared at us as if she didn't understand what she was seeing.

Alf rushed at her, running as fast as his legs could carry him. Binnie slipped through my grasp like an eel.

"Mama!"

"Mama!"

Their mother grabbed them as they leapt into her arms. She clenched them to her, sobbing, then began frantically kissing the tops of their heads.

Tom made a slight, throat-clearing sound, and I stepped on his foot. I didn't want to hear any of his scornful comments right now.

But the woman heard him. She looked up sharply, still clutching her children. Her face was tear-streaked and grim.

"You," she said to Tom.

"Madam Isabella." Tom swept into a graceful bow. "You're looking well. Prison agrees with you."

"You *know* her?" I said.

"Oh yes," Tom said. "She was the only human in this town who thought, from the beginning, that I was worse than a plague of rats." He inclined his head respectfully in her direction. "She attempted to convince the others to run me out of town."

Alf tried to turn around. His mother pulled him even tighter. "We'd all be better off if I had succeeded."

"I wouldn't say that," Tom murmured.

She narrowed her eyes.

"I mean," Tom said primly, "just because something is true, is no reason to say it."

Madam Isabella got to her feet. She had to let go of her children to do so, and both of them wrapped their arms around her legs. She had started stepping toward us, but now she couldn't move, so she folded her arms across her chest instead. "I think you'll find that most people have come around to my point of view. If I were you, I wouldn't prolong your stay here."

I waited for Tom to reply. When he didn't, I cleared my throat. "I brought your children back, like you asked."

Alf and Binnie were miraculously quiet, their faces buried in their mother's skirt. She looked down at them. "Yes. Thank you." When she looked up, I saw that her eyes were rimmed with red. "But I can't help noticing that you also brought the person who stole them to begin with."

I looked sideways at Tom and put every bit of hope I had into my voice. "He won't do it again."

Tom smiled widely and stretched his arms above his head. "I'll be going to get some sleep now. Your children are quite exhausting, and I don't want to be too tired to enjoy the festival tomorrow." He turned on his heel and walked off.

My legs twitched. But instead of following him I stood in the doorway, staring down at the packed dirt. I felt Tom leave more than I heard it. His footsteps were feather light, but the air around me seemed duller and heavier in his absence. My whole body felt hollowed out.

"Right, then," Madam Isabella said. "Let's go home." She gently pushed Alf and Binnie away from her—then, when they refused to move, a little less gently. "You both need dinner and bed."

"But no bath," Binnie said. "I DON'T need a bath. I NEVER—" She broke off as her mother grabbed her under the arms and swung her upward.

"Wait!" Alf said. "I want Clare to come with us."

My head jerked up.

"Yeah!" Binnie said. "Me too! *Please,* Mama?"

Their mother regarded me over the top of Binnie's head. Her expression was extremely unfriendly. It occurred to me, too late, that it might have been safer to go with Tom.

"She's the one who got the Piper to bring us back," Alf said.

Madam Isabella's expression shifted. She studied me carefully. "Is that so?"

"I SAID it was!" Alf shouted, highly insulted.

"And what," Madam Isabella asked me, "do you intend to do with the children now?"

"Nothing!" I said. "I want *you* to keep your children."

That made her smile for just a second. Maybe I had said it a little too vehemently.

"But"—I swallowed hard—"that's not what my brother wants." It made me sick to the stomach to say it. "I want to stop him. And I need help."

Madam Isabella glanced swiftly at Alf, then back at me. "Stop him how?"

"I don't know." I hesitated. "Yet."

She pursed her lips. Binnie flung her arms around her mother's neck, and Madam Isabella seemed to come to a decision. She put Binnie down. "Why don't you come eat dinner with us, and we can talk."

"I want *cake* for dinner!" Binnie said. "Like in the cave!"

"That's ridiculous," Alf said. "Humans can't have cake for—OW! Mama! She *kicked* me!"

"Well," Madam Isabella amended, "we can talk once they're asleep."

"I'm not *tired*!" Alf shouted, and Binnie burst into tears.

Madam Isabella looked at them, then at me. "I really am grateful to you for bringing them home."

I grabbed Binnie's arm before she could punch Alf. "I'm sure you are."

———◆———

Dinner was bland, the way most human food is, but I was hungry enough to clear my plate anyway. Binnie refused to eat a bite, because, she explained, she intended to eat only cake from now on. There followed a prolonged discussion between Alf and Binnie of the merits of her plan, carried out at the top of their lungs, that ended with Alf refusing to eat his food until Binnie ate hers.

All the while, I tried to figure out a way to change Tom's mind. I couldn't think of a single plan that might work. I couldn't even think of one that I could convince myself might work.

Luckily, Madam Isabella didn't say anything about Tom during dinner. Maybe she didn't want her children to understand that their safety was only temporary.

Finally, dinner ended. I sat alone at the table while

Madam Isabella tucked Alf and Binnie into bed. Madam Isabella's home was much smaller than the mayor's or the prison; it was basically one large room occupied mostly by a rectangular wooden table with two rough-hewn benches on either side of it. A set of stairs led up to the loft where they slept. I got up and looked out one of the windows, watching stripes of dusky purple and orange streak along the horizon.

A face popped up on the other side of the window.

I screamed. Anna flinched and put a finger to her lips.

Too late. Madam Isabella came clumping down the stairs, while Alf screamed from above, "WHAT IS IT? WHAT HAPPENED?" and Binnie shouted, "I'M NOT TUCKED IN YET! MY BLANKET IS TWISTED!"

"I'm sorry!" I said. Madam Isabella held an iron rod in one hand like a weapon. "I was just startled by ... um ..."

"By me," Anna said from the other side of the window. "I'm here to help."

"WHO'S THERE? I WANT TO COME DOWN!"

"I CAN'T UNTWIST IT!"

"Stay in bed!" Madam Isabella shouted. She gave Anna a disgruntled look, leaned the iron rod against the wall, and pounded back up to the loft.

"Let me in," Anna whispered.

It wasn't my house. But Madam Isabella had seen Anna and then put down her weapon. I had no idea what human etiquette was for such situations.

"Quick!" Anna said, and disappeared from the window.

I bit my lower lip. Did I even want Anna's help, now that I knew she had been lying to me this whole time?

But even as I thought it, I was crossing the room. When I pulled the door open, Anna quickly stepped inside. She was still wearing the clothes she'd had on when we left Hamelin, and her matted and tangled hair was plastered to her head.

"I'm sorry," she said. "But there's something you need to know. Please listen to me."

I stepped back so she could get to the table, and I shut the door behind her. Really, how could I blame Anna for lying to me? I had stood by my brother even after he kidnapped the town's children. I couldn't expect Anna to do any less for her father.

Madam Isabella came back down the stairs. She didn't seem upset to see Anna inside the house, which hopefully meant I'd made the right decision. She went straight to the table, her hair straggling out of the tight bun she'd tied it into before dinner, and sat at the end of one bench.

"I don't have much time." Anna spoke fast. "I have to get back before my father notices I'm gone. But you said it might help if you knew what Tom bargained for."

"It's the only hope we have left," I said. Madam Isabella flinched, and I realized I probably shouldn't have said that. I went on. "If I know what he wants, maybe I can find another way to get it for him. Then he won't need to take the children. Do you have a way to find out what he bargained for?"

Anna was silent for a moment, two bright spots of color on her cheeks. Then she said, "I don't have to find out. I know."

"*You* know?" I said. "How would you know?"

Anna twisted her fingers together. "I'm sorry," she said. "I should have told you earlier. I shouldn't have done it. I just . . . I didn't know what would happen. I didn't think about what would happen."

"What are you talking about?" I demanded.

Anna took a deep breath.

"The bargain wasn't Tom's idea," she said. "It was mine."

25

Outside the window, the sky had faded to a murky gray-black. Alf's and Binnie's snores drifted down the stairs. The air in the room was so still I couldn't hear anyone breathe.

Madam Isabella broke the silence. "That can't be," she said to Anna. She spoke gently, as if to a hysterical child.

"It was after the time I spent in the Realms." Anna looked at me intently. I wondered how much of my expression she could make out in the dim light. "When Tom came to take me home, I begged him to let me stay. I could see how worried he was about you, so I suggested a trade: you for me."

One human girl for one fae princess. Not a fair trade, as far as my mother would have been concerned.

"He went to the queen. I didn't realize . . . I didn't know she was going to ask for more children. All I offered was myself. But Tom made a different deal."

"When did you figure it out?" I demanded.

"Not until I woke in the wagon." Her voice was so low I could barely hear her. "My father and the other members of the town council took us there while we were sleeping. I think they must have given us sleeping draughts, because when I woke in the morning, the rest of the children were still asleep. And then ... you know what happened then."

Then she had sneaked out of the wagon and made her way back to Hamelin, where she had interrupted my disastrous rescue attempt. That was why her father had been startled to see her. That was why she had been so disheveled.

And then she had joined my quest. But she hadn't done it to help me get the children back.

She had intended to join them.

"I tried to tell you," Anna said. "But I was ashamed. And I told Tom afterward, in the caves, that I wanted to back out of the bargain. But he said it was too late. That it wasn't about me anymore."

"It was never about you," I said.

How had she not realized? How had *I* not realized?

There was only one person for whom Tom would risk so much. Only one reason he would dare the queen's wrath, make unwise alliances, and put his position at court in jeopardy.

It had always, always been about me.

"He's trying to get me out of the Realms," I said. I turned to Madam Isabella. "That's why he took your children. He was trading them for me." I put one hand on the table, my legs rubbery. "I'm sorry. I'm so, so sorry. But now that I know what he's trying to do, I know how to stop it."

"How?" Madam Isabella asked.

"I'll tell him I won't go. That I'll stay in the Realms no matter what. Then he'll have nothing to gain from taking the children."

Madam Isabella gave me a long look. "And he won't take them anyhow? The fae don't need a reason to steal children, do they?"

"Tom's not fae. Not really."

The fae are good at lying. But humans don't even know when they're lying.

"He'll be at the festival tomorrow," I said. "I'll talk to him then."

Madam Isabella passed a hand over her eyes. A muscle jumped in her cheek, and I wondered if she believed me.

But all she said was, "Do you need a place to sleep tonight?"

I tensed instinctively. No fae issued an invitation without winding it around a trick.

"I don't mean to offend," she added. She seemed

completely sincere. "I've heard that the fae don't like sleeping under roofs."

In the Realms, that was true. But I had discovered over the past few weeks that there were *numerous* advantages to sleeping under a roof. I looked around at the warm, crowded room and the dishes still strewn on the table. Soft snores drifted down from the loft.

"Thank you," I said. "But I have some things to take care of first."

———◆———

My bond with Tom didn't work outside the Realms, but he hadn't gone far. He was already asleep when I found him, lying on his side on a grassy spot near the edge of town, surrounded by crinkly, colorful leaves. Apparently, despite all his time in the human world, *he* had not yet discovered the advantages of roofs.

He had covered himself with a glamour that hid him from the townspeople, but I saw through it easily. I lay on the cold, wet grass next to him, ignoring the dampness that crept through my clothes.

The leaves rustled. Tom opened one eye and smiled at me, and I scooted closer. He draped an arm around me, the way he used to when we first came to the Realms, when we had huddled together in whatever safe space we could find.

"Don't worry," he murmured, just as he had back then. "I won't let anything happen to you."

"I know," I whispered back.

He sent his magic sliding under me, warm and dry, so it felt like I was resting on a soft blanket. The damp leached away from my clothes.

"Thank you," I said, and the corners of his mouth lifted slightly as his eyes closed.

I waited until his body was so immobile I couldn't tell whether he was breathing—the utter stillness of fae sleep. I rolled out from under his arm onto the damp ground and reached into his cloak. I slid my hand into three pockets before I found what I was looking for.

I looked at my brother's face, so peaceful and cold. *He's not fae*, I had said—and when I'd said it, I'd believed it. I had been thinking of the Tom I remembered, the brother who had always been by my side, as human and alone as I was.

For so long, I had held on to the memory of that human boy who had followed me into the Realms to protect me. I hadn't wanted to see what it had cost him; how he'd had to learn the faes' ways, understand their thoughts, to keep me safe. Tom had made himself what he was, had shifted gradually into one of them, for *me*.

But that didn't change the fact that he was what he was.

The pipe felt as surprisingly light as it had in the caves. I resisted the urge to blow into it. I got to my feet and walked away from my sleeping brother, not trying to be quiet. When it comes to the fae, you are *more* likely to wake them with stealth. That was one of the first things Tom taught me.

All my life, I had wished to be more like Tom. To be canny and unafraid and powerful like him, despite all the cruelty and strangeness that surrounded us. He had always protected me, and I had always known I couldn't survive without him. Not in the Realms. I was too human.

I was human because Tom had kept me human. Because I had grown up being loved by him.

When I reached the river, I hesitated. The current was black and flat and deceptively still, except for the constant, rushing murmur between its banks.

I aimed for the deepest part.

The pipe hit the water with a splash, and for a moment I thought it would sink. Instead it bobbed to the surface, whirled once in a froth of bubbles, then streamed with the dark current around the curve of the river and out of sight.

26

When I woke the next morning, a large, hawklike bird was circling overhead, so close I could see individual feathers jutting from its outspread wings. I watched it balance on the wind, then turned to see if Tom had also noticed it.

The space next to me was empty. There was only a flattened patch of grass where he had been.

I blinked hard to keep the tears from coming. Then I got to my feet and headed for the town square.

Music drifted through the air, but it wasn't the sound of the pipe; it was a thin, thready tune, interrupted frequently by stamping feet and raucous cheers. I had slept late. The sun was high over the horizon, only a few ragged wisps of sunrise left in the sky. The festival had already begun.

By the time I got to the square, the bird had

disappeared. Perhaps it had only been a hawk or a vulture that had found no prey and moved on.

Perhaps.

The townspeople had attempted to transform the square into a merry, colorful place. Lines of patchwork cloth were draped from rooftop to rooftop, and the scattered stone basins were filled with fresh flowers. (Well, they were mostly weeds. But colorful weeds.) Rows of wooden benches lined one side of the square; on the other side were rickety stalls with various games and refreshments. On the central stone platform, a fiddler played an instrument badly in need of tuning while townspeople stamped and waved their arms around him in uncoordinated motions that vaguely resembled a dance. I paused on the outskirts of the square, looking at the dancers, but I didn't see Tom or Anna among them.

It wasn't at all like a faerie ball. Everything was clumsy and plain, the air was unpleasantly damp, and the people smelled of sweat and dirt. Also, someone had already eaten too much and thrown up in the grass.

I stepped up onto a low rock wall, searching the crowd. I still saw no sign of Tom or Anna—or of Madam Isabella. But the people were so closely packed, and moving so swiftly, that I could easily have missed them.

Most of the adults were dancing, but the children

sat in clusters on the benches. Their small faces were scrubbed, their clothes not yet stained. A surprising rush of warmth went through me, and I thought about going over to check on them.

"I can't *see!*" a familiar voice shouted. "Let me through!"

"Stop pushing!" another child yelled, and there was a thud whose origin I couldn't identify.

On second thought . . .

I made my way to the stalls and stopped at the nearest one, where a woman was dipping a pair of tongs into a large pot hung over a fire. The scent of boiling oil made my eyes water.

"Excuse me," I said. "I'm looking for Anna, the mayor's daughter."

The woman's head snapped up. The oil sizzled and popped, and it occurred to me that the mayor might already have had time to turn the townspeople against me. And also that those tongs were made of metal and burning hot. I reached for the magic I'd gathered in the Realms, but most of it had already dissipated.

"You're the Pied Piper's sister," she said. "The one that went after the children."

I forced myself not to back away.

She reached behind her and plucked something off a tray. She held it out to me: a round, doughy thing soaked in oil.

"You look like you just woke up," she said. "Would you like a doughnut for breakfast?"

"Er—thank you." I took the round piece of dough. Then, since she was watching me, I bit into it.

Oh. *Oh.* It tasted almost like food from the Realms.

"Another?" she suggested.

I looked down at my empty, oily hands and realized that I had eaten the entire doughnut.

"That's how you thank her for bringing our children back?" Another woman laughed from behind me. "By giving her a stomachache?"

The first woman grinned. "Some harvest bread instead?"

"No, thank you." I'd had harvest bread last night at Madam Isabella's. It tasted like sawdust. (Alf's word. But the child was right.)

You've been spoiled by faerie food, Madam Isabella had snapped at him. *Best get used to human food again, because that's what you'll be getting from now on.*

And then she had caught herself and looked at me, terror and hope mingled in her eyes.

"I'm looking for the mayor's daughter," I said. "Do you know where she is?"

"She's not here," the woman behind me said. She had a toddler propped up on her hip, a little boy with a harelip who had spent most of yesterday whining that his feet hurt. He looked at me with round, solemn eyes, his feet dangling several feet above the ground. "I heard the mayor locked her in her room last night, he was that worried for her safety. But he'll probably bring her to the festival when he comes."

So the mayor wasn't here yet. I breathed a bit easier and said cautiously, "Are you sure her father will allow her to come?"

The women exchanged glances. "Who knows?" the doughnut maker said, plucking another doughnut out of the pot and turning to place it on the tray behind her. "Nothing he's ever done to control her has worked. After everything that happened, no one would blame him if he kept her under guard until all this is over."

"No one will blame him for much of anything now," the other woman added.

I blinked at her. "Why not?"

"Well," she said, "he got rid of the rats, didn't he? *And* he got our children back. So it all worked out. He even has a plan for how to keep it from happening again."

It was a moment before I could speak. "*He* didn't get the children back! I did!"

"Didn't he force you to?"

"No!"

"Really? He told us he had an iron wristband ready that he could use to force the fae."

"Well ... he did ..."

"Didn't he put it on you?"

"Yes, but. ... it's more complicated than—"

"DOUGHNUT!" the toddler shouted, and grabbed his mother's hair. Glad for the distraction, I backed away from the stall.

"Clare!" a familiar voice called, and Alf pulled my skirt. "Come dance!"

"Um—" I said, but he was already pulling me in among the dancers.

The dance steps were fast and unfamiliar, so I kept bumping into people, and the music was so off-key that I couldn't use it as a guide. After a few minutes, Alf let go of me and raced off to find some other amusement, and a woman with extremely sweaty hands grabbed me and pulled me into a circle of dancers.

The dancers changed direction without warning, yanking my arms painfully. I wrenched free and backed away, and the circle closed in front of me, two women joining hands as if I had never been there.

The doughnut I had eaten twisted into a hard, nauseating lump in the pit of my stomach. I didn't belong here. I had danced on beams of moonlight in magic slippers. I had been possessed by unearthly music, had soared effortlessly through moon-soaked air and landed lightly as a breeze, had tilted my head back to drink water as sweet as liquid sugar. And I had done all those things with Tom watching, smiling to see me happy, vigilant to keep me safe.

I wondered if I would ever see him again.

I spotted a girl with white-blond hair and opened my mouth to call Anna's name, but then the girl turned and she was actually an older woman. Behind her, I caught a glimpse of a wiry young boy with slick black hair; I blinked and stopped moving for a second, but the dancers shifted and I couldn't get a second look. Someone stepped on my foot. I yelped, then yelped again as something small and furry brushed my ankle. I looked down just in time to see a rat race past the doughnut stall and out of the square.

It might have been an ordinary rat. Except it hadn't stopped to snatch up any of the pieces of doughnut that had been trodden underfoot.

I struggled through the dancers and raced after it.

The doughnut maker glanced at me as I rushed past her stall. From the corner of my eye, I saw other heads turn. But no one tried to stop or question me. Perhaps they thought I was leaving for good.

Perhaps they were glad of that. I would have been, if I were them.

But the rat did not lead me back toward the corn-fields and the mountain. It turned at the entrance to the town and scampered off the road, darting between low bushes and rocks. I followed it through brambles and high, hard grass, only realizing after several minutes that it was leading me toward the river.

The river was gray and flat in the sunlight, long, muted ripples interrupted by the occasional white splash. By the time I reached it, I had lost track of the rat . . . but I could see why it had led me here. A giant rat crouched on a rock by the bank, gnawing on a bone. He turned his head and waggled his whiskers at me.

I stopped walking, swiping at the tiny insects that buzzed eagerly around me. Downriver, the current was broken up by a cluster of gray boulders that sent the water leaping over and around them in frantic whirls of white froth. This was where Tom had drowned all of Per's subjects . . . except that had been a ruse, too; the rats must have managed to avoid the boulders and swim underwater to the caves. For all I knew, many of them were still under that silvery current, waiting for me.

But Per didn't look angry. His tail was draped across the rock, and he licked one paw extensively before focusing on me. "That was quite the betrayal," he said. "Stealing the pipe from your brother's pocket while he slept? I have to admit, I didn't think you had it in you. Neither did Tom."

My stomach twisted. I glanced again at the water. The sunlight turned it into a gleam of white sparkles.

"I had no choice," I said. "I had to stop him."

Per rubbed his teeth together, making a purring sound. "Do you really think you stopped him?"

"No," I admitted. Something stung my wrist. I slapped at it and missed. "But at least I've delayed him. He won't be taking these children today."

Per fixed his beady eyes on me. "Are you sure of that?"

"He can't. He doesn't have the—" I stopped. Per was so smug his eyes were literally bulging out. I looked at the river, then back at him, and my fingernails cut ridges into my palms.

"It wasn't a bad attempt," Per said generously. "But the pipe got caught in some tree roots about a league downriver. Some of my nimbler subjects were able to retrieve it."

It took me a moment to find my voice. "Why would you help him? I thought you would be glad to see him disgraced! You said your partnership was over."

"That was then." Per grinned, revealing long, curved yellow teeth. "*Now* he owes me several favors, which I intend to collect. He'll grow in power at court once he pulls this off, and those favors will be quite valuable."

He wrapped his tail around his hind legs. "Especially since you were his only weakness, and he's finally managed to get rid of you."

"He has *not*," I said.

Per twisted to lick his hindquarters. "By nightfall, the children will belong to the queen. You can't stop it. If you really loved your brother, you wouldn't want to." He smirked. "Tell Anna that when she comes to the Realms, I will be waiting for her. Tell her that I would wait forever for her."

"I will not!"

He laughed. "I'd go tell her myself, but I think we're out of time." He slid down the rock and into the river in one quick motion. A line of white froth followed him as he paddled toward the other side.

He swam silently, and all was still but for the constant, rushing murmur of the current.

Until, a moment later, I heard what Per had: the high, lilting call of the pipe drifting through the morning air.

27

I turned and ran away from the river, brambles ripping at my calves. I reached the road just in time to see Tom striding down its center, heading toward Hamelin. His cloak billowed behind him, a riot of colors, and the silver pipe flashed in the sunlight.

The tune he played was one I hadn't heard before, low and long and flat. That vision of gigantic purple and yellow flowers filled my mind, but only for a second. I shook off the pipe's effects, and then I saw who else had been affected: children were streaming from the town, dancing and twirling down the road toward my brother.

I braced myself as Tom got near. But he walked past me as if he didn't see me.

I stood there, feeling as if I had been punched and knowing I had no right to expect anything better. Then I gathered myself and raced after him. I let the tune of the pipe spur me to greater speed, to help overcome the tiny, shameful part of me that wanted to turn and run the other way. I reached Tom, grabbed his colorful cloak, and yanked.

He whirled to face me. The motion sent me staggering off-balance, and I fell onto the dirt road with a thud I felt all the way up my spine. My brother stood over me and lowered the pipe from his lips.

"Hello, Clare," he said.

I scuttled backward, then scrambled to my feet. I had to tilt my head back to meet Tom's eyes, and his shadow stretched much farther along the ground than mine did.

"I'm sorry, Tom," I said. "I had to do it."

He smiled without showing his teeth and twirled the pipe between his fingers. "You did delay me," he said. "So if that was your intent, you succeeded. I had to wait a while for the pipe to dry. But now, as you see, it's good as new." He lifted it to his lips and blew a short, peremptory trill.

"Don't," I said desperately. "I know why you're doing this, Tom. I know it's for me. Anna told me about the bargain she suggested."

"She's so adorable, isn't she?" Tom tossed the pipe in the air, spinning it in a slow circle and catching it easily. His fury was smooth as ice. Like our mother's anger, it showed only in the flat coldness of his voice. "One human girl for one fae princess. She honestly thought the queen would agree to that."

I tried to feel angry, too. "But *you* didn't think so, did you? You knew she would ask for the whole town's children."

"She asked for several towns' children," Tom corrected me. "I bargained her down to one." He folded his arms across his chest, the pipe dangling from his hand. "Not that I cared. But I knew you would. And I did all of this for you."

That wasn't anger in his voice after all. It was hurt.

Which made me feel even worse.

"I needed to get you out of the Realms." Tom's jaw tightened. "You're too human to survive there. I was constantly rescuing you. You're older now than I was when we first entered the Realms, and you still couldn't manage to protect yourself. And then, when I saw how you were with Anna, I couldn't deny it anymore. You were never going to like it there."

It had never occurred to me that *liking it* was an option. Which was, perhaps, why I had failed to notice that Tom *did* like it there.

He played another trill on the pipe, keeping the spell going. "When you tracked me down in the caves, all by yourself, I thought—I hoped I was wrong. I almost changed my mind."

Until I had changed it back. I had insisted that I was human—had yelled it at him—right before he decided to take me back to Hamelin.

That was what Tom had heard, what had made him change tack and redouble his efforts to get me out. It had nothing to do with some random other human children he didn't care about. It had to do with his sister, his too-human sister who would never be happy in the Realms because it wasn't where she belonged.

The children were still coming; they were so close now I could make out their faces. Alf was holding Binnie's hand. The boy who'd had the stomachache was carrying the toddler with the harelip. I didn't see Anna, and for a moment I thought her father had successfully kept her locked in her room. Then two children danced apart and Anna pushed her way to the head of the pack, her cane sweeping the ground in front of her. She was wearing the same clothes as before, her hair still matted to her face. She looked like she hadn't slept since we got back to Hamelin.

There were other children, ones I didn't recognize. A chubby boy who looked a lot like the mayor's mustached henchman, except the black bristles of hair were on top of his head instead of on his face. A pretty girl in fine silks, her hair tied up in a dozen braids.

All the children were here this time. I wondered if

their parents were still dancing in the square, oblivious to what was happening, the pipe's music holding them in place rather than summoning them. That would be extremely advanced magic. But not out of the question for a fae prince who was willing to expend every bit of power and influence he had to save his human sister.

Tom played another quick tune on the pipe, and the children pushed themselves to go even faster.

"Tom, stop." My breath hurt coming into my chest. "I won't let you do this."

His eyes glittered. "Won't *let* me?"

"I'm not staying here," I said. "If you take these children, I'll come back to the Realms with them. You won't have gained anything."

Tom's eyes narrowed. His cheekbones cast shadows so stark they looked like bruises. I felt a flash of the fear that I usually only felt around our mother.

"I mean it." My voice shook so hard that my words were almost unintelligible, but I knew Tom understood me. "I know you made the bargain in order to get me out. But I'm coming back no matter what you do. So you don't need these children. Let them go."

"No matter what I do?" Tom said. "I don't think you've thought this through, Clare."

His lips curved into a smile around the pipe's mouthpiece. He turned and stepped off the road, light and graceful, striding right past me and down the hill's slope.

Toward the vast gray rush of the river.

It took me several seconds to grasp what he was doing. It was only when Anna passed me that I understood. I rushed ahead of her and grabbed my brother's cloak again. This time, I held on until he stopped and turned. By then we were nearly at the riverbank, and the air around us buzzed with tiny insects.

"No," I said. "Tom, *no*. You wouldn't."

The rush and murmur of the river filled my ears, but Tom's voice cut through it clearly. "Like you said, if you're coming with me, I don't need them." His eyes were black and cold. "If you want me to take them to the Realms, then you stay behind. Otherwise I'll lead them straight into the water. Every last one."

The fae can lie. The fae can lie. He was bluffing.

But I wasn't sure he was.

I stepped back from my brother, mud sucking at my feet. He watched me with a small, cruel smile: a fae prince, cold and calculating and heartless. The only thing that made him different from any of the other fae was that he loved his little sister.

Which wasn't a difference that mattered at all when it came to the fate of Hamelin's children.

Anna caught up to us a few feet ahead of the others.

She had an advantage: none of the children could see the rough terrain hidden by the tall grass, and she had her cane to help her. Her jaw was set, and I wondered if she was fighting the call of the pipe. She wouldn't be able to fight for long, though. None of them would, not even when the water closed over their heads.

"All right," I said. My breath was a solid block in my throat, and I had to force my words out around it. "You win, Tom. You take the children to the Realms and I'll stay here." I grabbed Anna's arm, trying to drag her back from the river. She fought to get free. "Make them *stop!*"

Tom blew a shatteringly sharp note on the pipe. All at once, Anna stopped fighting me. She turned to stare at Tom, her chest heaving. The other children stumbled to a stop as well, watching my brother with eager eyes.

Tom flicked his cloak into a swirl of colors.

"I'll do it," I said desperately. "I'll go back."

"I wouldn't go *back*," Tom said. "Hamelin might not be the best place for you at the moment. Maybe go somewhere else."

"Thank you," I snarled. "That's excellent advice."

His smile flickered. When it returned, it was tinged with sadness, which made him look almost human. "Don't be angry, Clare. I'm doing what's best for you. And the children will be happy enough in the Realms."

There was no point in saying anything, so I didn't.

"I'll take care of them," he added.

"No," I said. "You won't." I turned from him and pulled Anna's arm. "*You'll* have to take care of them. Do you understand? You can't count on Tom."

"Clare, no." Anna's voice was rough and halting. "There has to be another way."

"I won't forget you," I said. "I'll find a way to come after you. I'll bring you back, all of you—"

My voice cracked. Sometimes, it's harder to lie when you're human.

I reached forward and pulled Anna into a hug.

Her body remained stiff, but her arms came up and her fingers dug into my back. Wetness dripped onto my shoulders. She was sobbing so hard she didn't notice when I dipped my hand into her pocket.

Burning tingles went up my fingers, which was useful. The pain made tears spring to my eyes, and when I pulled back, they were running down my cheeks. I turned to my brother, whose face softened. He stepped forward and swiped one finger along my cheek, wiping it dry.

That was when, in one swift movement, I snapped the iron band around his wrist.

28

Tom screamed.

His scream went on and on, and there was nothing human about it. I had heard fae scream like that, in frustration and rage, when their will was thwarted. If I hadn't been staring straight at him, I would not have known that sound of anguished fury was coming from my brother.

He fell over, landing on his side, and the pipe dropped from his hand. It hit the ground and rolled, coming to rest against a rock. He banged his wrist against the ground as if he could knock the iron band free, groaning in uneven guttural bursts.

The iron band had hurt me, too, but not as much as it hurt someone who was almost fully fae. Tom's jaw clenched. Then he screamed again, and I knew he had tried to use his magic.

I couldn't bear it. I dropped to my knees next to

him. He was curled up in a ball, not moving, his eyes squeezed shut.

Then I saw his fist clenched against his chest, his pinkie finger sticking out. The signal he had taught me, the way I let him know I needed him to take my magic.

I grabbed his hand. My fingers didn't fit all the way around his, but it didn't matter. He let out a gasp as his magic burst through my skin.

He had so much of it—as much as any true fae. It nearly knocked me backward as it rushed through my blood in a torrent of fire, too much for my small human body.

I forced myself to keep my hand on Tom's, pressing my fingertips against his knuckles as the magic poured out of him and into me. I held on to it for just a second longer than I should have, feeling it fill me with power and possibility.

Then I let it go.

The colors exploded from me, fierce and bright, millions of sparkles that arced above the river. Here there were no cave walls to catch them, so they just kept going: out and out, bursting into lines and waves and, finally, into a rainbow-colored mist. They filled the sky with shifting, colorful light. Each time one color dissipated, a new one burst from where it had been, dancing around and through and within each other, swirling among the silent, staring children on the riverbank.

Colors they had never seen. Colors they still didn't see.

They stood watching, eyes wide with wonder. Their faces, lit by the shifting colors, looked almost fae.

I used the last bit of magic to call the pipe. It flew straight into my hand, and its power met the magic in my skin with a burst that I felt throughout my body.

Then it was gone, and most of the colors disappeared from my sight. I watched the remaining colors, the human ones, grow fainter and farther away.

Tom sat up beside me, his face clear, his eyes dark. His arm was burned red all the way up to the shoulder, and the skin around the iron band was black.

He looked frightened and furious and completely human. I hadn't seen him look this human for a very long time.

"Well," he said. "It seems you're capable of even more than I thought. Perhaps we should rethink whether you could thrive in the Realms."

I kept my eyes on my knuckles, clenched white against the silver pipe. "Go," I said. "Go back to the Realms. You'll have to tell Mother you failed."

"It's not that simple," Tom said. His voice was expressionless. "You know you can't escape a bargain with the queen."

"It was *your* bargain." I finally looked up at him. "Not mine."

He blinked. To my surprise, he didn't look angry. He looked confused.

"Don't you see?" I said. "I don't have to obey her when I'm outside her kingdom."

He stared at me as if I was speaking a foreign language. Which I was, to anyone who had grown up in the Realms. Everybody had to obey the queen.

Anna hadn't, though, when she kicked her way out of her prison. And I hadn't, when I played the pipe in the caves. Because humans . . .

Humans, she had to bargain with.

"Why do you think she made me promise to bring the pipe back?" I said. "Why did she say she would teach me to play it? Because she knew I didn't *have* to come back. She had to try to convince me, because she couldn't force me."

"She's the queen," Tom said blankly.

"And I'm human. I'm not under her control, and I never was. You bargained for her to let me out. That bargain wasn't fulfilled, yet here I am. Nobody had to *let* me out. I left on my own." I took a deep breath. "I left to find you."

"And you found me," Tom said.

"Yes," I agreed. "I did."

The pipe hummed in my hand. I could tell by the way Tom leaned forward that he wanted to grab it. Too late, I wondered if I should have kept some of his magic.

But all he did was shake his head. "Imagine that," he said. "You didn't need me to get you out. You didn't need me at all."

"You know that's not true. I still need you. For one thing, I did promise Mother I'd return her pipe." I peeled my fingers away from the cool silver and placed the pipe in Tom's palm. "Give it back to her for me."

My brother looked at the pipe. He glanced around at the children, still enthralled by the fading magic. His fingers closed around the pipe, and every muscle in my body went tense.

He lifted an eyebrow. "Do you expect me to go back to the Realms with iron shackled to my wrist?"

"Of course not." I turned to Anna and held out my hand.

She hesitated. "Are you sure . . . ?"

"He won't take the children," I said. "He doesn't need them anymore."

She glanced at Tom, bit her lip, then pulled the key out of her pocket and handed it to me.

I knelt next to my brother. My fingers shook so much it took me two tries to slide the key in.

Never, ever get close to an angry fae.

I turned the key and released the band. It fell to the ground with a soft thud.

Tom surged up and forward. His arms went around me, and I closed my eyes and hugged him back, my cheek pressed against one of the buttons on his cloak. It was a square button, and it hurt, but I didn't draw away until I felt his grip loosen. Then I uncurled my fingers from his shirt and stepped back. I could feel how wet my face was, but I didn't care.

Tom wasn't crying—the fae don't—but his face was somber, his eyes dark with a grief I had never seen in the Realms. Had never seen until the day I walked into Hamelin's grim streets, gray and lifeless without its children.

"It won't be this easy," he warned. "Mother won't like it. She'll be angry at me—don't worry, I can manage that—but she'll be even angrier at you."

"Then I guess you'll have to think of ways to distract her." I tried to smile. "I still need you to keep me safe."

Tom's voice was so low I could barely make out what he said. "Clare. Once I'm fully fae, I won't want to anymore."

"You know what?" I said. "I think you're wrong about that."

His eyes were fathomless pools. "You're what's kept

me human, Clare. Once I stop loving you, I'll be just like the rest of them."

"I'm not worried about that," I said. "You'll never stop loving me."

"You know better." He drew his shoulders together. His arm was healed, skin smooth and unmarred. "The fae don't love."

I *did* know that. Which was how I knew my brother would never be fully fae.

But I supposed he'd have to figure that out on his own.

"Goodbye, Tom," I said.

Tom looked once more at the children and sighed regretfully, the way he always did when I got stubborn over something he considered ridiculous. "I hope they'll at least pay you for bringing back the children. I was planning to send you with a chest full of gold coins."

I'd spent enough time in the human world to understand how useful that would have been. But I shrugged. "I'll manage. Don't worry."

A thin, high call sounded above. I looked up. A bird flew high overhead, heading toward the mountain in a straight, determined line, until it was nothing but a tiny black shape against the bright blue sky.

Tom whirled in a flash of gaudy colors. When he reached the road, he glanced back at me and grinned, the familiar warm smile he had only ever shown to me.

Then he started up the road, his colorful cloak billowing behind him, and I stood with the children of Hamelin and watched him go.

⇛ EPILOGUE ⇚

The next time I heard the pipe's music, I was elbow-deep in ballots.

It was the second batch of ballots. The first set had been involved in an unfortunate incident involving glue, scissors, and either Alf or Binnie, depending on which one you asked. (If you asked me, it was both of them.)

The music drifted through the cottage's window, which was decorated with the pink and purple patchwork curtains Anna and I had made. I put the scissors down, lunged across the table, and grabbed Alf by the arm before he could move. He blinked at me.

"What are you doing?" he said. He sat perfectly still—well, as still as he ever sat—giving no indication that he was about to leap to his feet and start dancing.

That was when I realized I was the only one who could hear the music.

I let go of Alf, who shrugged philosophically and went back to lettering the last pile of ballots. Spelling the names wrong, I might add; I would have to redo them later. Luckily, we still had days to go before the election.

You might think, after everything that had happened, that Mayor Herman would have been run out of town. You'd think wrong. Most people were fairly confused about what had actually taken place when the Pied Piper came back, and the mayor had managed to convince many of them that he was the one who had arranged for the children's return.

When I stepped into the front yard, I almost walked into Madam Isabella. She was pacing back and forth, practicing her speech for tomorrow's town hall. I had worked on the speech with her for hours, convincing her to take out the parts where she explained to the townspeople what fools they had been and then asked them to vote for her.

"Once you're mayor," Anna had said, "then you can call them fools."

I was *almost* sure she was joking. I was completely sure Madam Isabella didn't know she was joking.

Madam Isabella paused in the middle of the word *nincompoop* and lifted a questioning eyebrow at me. I hesitated. But the music coiled around my heart and urged my legs to move, so I merely waved, walked around her, and followed the sound of the pipe down the street and into the town square.

A group of children were playing in the square, some complicated game that involved running and thumping people on the back. None of them glanced in the direction the music was coming from.

I realized then how easy it was for me to stand and listen. My feet didn't twitch with the need to dance, and the yearning in my heart wasn't magical. It was just mine.

This wasn't a summons. This was Tom letting me know he remembered me.

The sound of the pipe soared through the air. I closed my eyes. The tune hit a high note, and the old memory flashed through me: purple and yellow flowers at eye level, almost the same size as my tiny face. Tom's large hand closing around my wrist. And the sound of the pipe drawing us onward, into a life completely different from the one we might have had.

I had never questioned the story I grew up with, of how I had wandered into the Realms by accident and my brother had followed me. But I knew now that it hadn't happened that way. In that earliest memory, the sound of the pipe had drawn me forward.

It had been no accident. We had been *summoned*.

But the summons had not been aimed at me, a use-less toddler without the strength to fulfill the queen's will. It had been Tom the queen had called for, Tom she had wanted. Tom she had traded for, so many years ago that I would never know what we had been traded for. *Tom* had been the first child of Hamelin to follow that call over the border, into a world of magic and danger.

I had been the one who followed *him*.

In the end, I supposed, it didn't really matter. Whether he had followed me over the border or taken me into the Realms with him, he'd done it for the same reason: to protect me.

And he was letting me know that I could still count on him to do that.

He was also telling me that he was all right. If he was playing the pipe so openly, that meant he wasn't in hid-ing, which meant our mother wasn't angry at him. I tried to imagine how Tom had pulled that off. Had he distracted her? Promised to bring her something new, as valuable as children? Directed her anger at some-one else?

I wished he would cross the border and tell me. Share gossip from the court, show me a magical arti-fact, take my hand and laugh with me. I reached in-stinctively for our bond, but of course I couldn't feel it. The sound of the pipe was the only hint to where he was.

"Clare?" Binnie said. I looked down, not sure when she had come to stand next to me. I hadn't even noticed she was in the square. "Are you sad?"

I looked at her bright face, then around the square, where children dashed between gray rocks and filled the chilly air with laughter. Anna was sitting on a low rock wall, swinging her legs back and forth. Beside her sat Grelda, another of my friends. Anna squinted across the square at me and lifted her hand in a small wave.

The pipe's tune soared, then plunged downward in a series of intricate trills. The notes didn't end so much as fade gently away, like a promise that they would soon resume.

"No," I said. "Not sad." I waved back at Anna. "Well, maybe a little sad. But mostly I'm happy."

I smiled to reassure Binnie. And then I kept smiling, humming the pipe's tune under my breath, as I turned and headed home.

Acknowledgments

The Pied Piper is unusual among fairy tales in that it is set in a specific time and place: the town of Hamelin, Germany, in (probably) the year 1284. Even though I didn't set my retelling in a historically accurate version of that place (for example: cornfields would not have existed in Europe until the sixteenth century), I benefited tremendously from the research that has been done on the Pied Piper story and its likely origins. The book *The Pied Piper: A Handbook* was my most invaluable resource. Every time I got stuck in the story, I would go back to reading that book, and within a couple of pages I would have half a dozen ideas for what might happen next. I am grateful to all the researchers whose interest in the tale has yielded such fascinating results, and to Wolfgang Mieder for compiling them.

When it came to the writing itself, I benefited, as always, from a cadre of stellar first readers and critique partners. My daughters, Shoshana and Hadassah, are first in line, as always; thanks also to Day al-Mohammed,

Christine Amsden, Chanie Beckman, LeahChaya Beilin, Sima Braunstein, Cécile Cristofari, Seth Z. Herman, Miriam Peromsik, Tova Suslovich, and Judith Tarr (for making sure the horses in chapter six behaved like actual horses).

I also greatly appreciate the people who helped me figure out Anna's limited vision—some directly, through critique and in discussion, and some indirectly, by creating books, magazines, and other resources for those who are part of the blind and low-vision community. (Needless to say, you are appreciated for more than just help with this particular book!) Any mistakes or inaccuracies that remain are entirely my own fault. I should note that Anna's white cane is another nonhistorical note in the story; while blind and partially sighted people have used canes to help get around for centuries, a specifically white cane—which not only helps people with low vision navigate their surroundings, but also indicates their blindness to other people—was introduced in the 1930s.

Thank you, as always, to everyone at Delacorte Press, including and especially Wendy Loggia and Ali Romig. Thanks also to Carol Ly and Maxine Vee for a beautiful cover, and to Lili Feinberg, Heather Lockwood Hughes, Nathan Kinney, Jade Rector, Lena Reilly, Tamar Schwartz, and Audrey Sussman.

Thank you to my fantastic agent, Andrea Somberg, and to my film agent, Mary Pender-Coplan at UTA.

Thank you to Josh Katz for the support and the pizza.

Thank you to my family: my husband, children, parents, siblings, in-laws, nieces, and nephews. While some of you will read this book enthusiastically the first chance you get, and some of you will get to it next time you're on a long flight, and some of you will never, ever open it . . . I know you're all in my corner, and it means a lot to me to have you there.

Meet Cinderella's third "evil" stepsister, Tirza, in

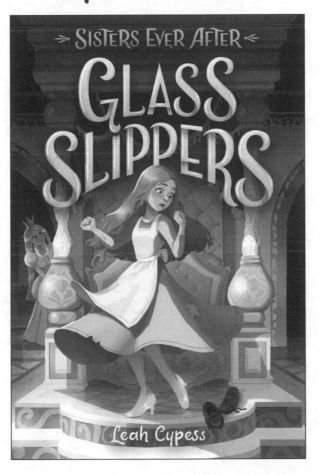

SISTERS EVER AFTER

GLASS SLIPPERS

Leah Cypess

Published by Delacorte Press, an imprint of Random House Children's Books,
a division of Penguin Random House LLC, New York.

1

My original plan for that day was *excellent*. It doesn't mean much now, but for the record, I want you to know how well things could have gone.

It was the morning of the annual parade. I planned to spend the day in the nursery playing with the royal princes. Queen Ella's children, Prince Baro and Prince Elrin, were also not allowed to go to the parade. They had begged me to come stay with them, and I had promised.

I would never break a promise to the princes. Even that time when I told Baro that if he went to sleep, I would sing him the entire ballad of *Sleeping Beauty* while standing on my head. I hadn't thought he would remember, but he had, and I'd done it. Gilma, their nursemaid, had caught me and told everyone, which had gone over really well with the court.

But the princes were the only people in the castle

who trusted me, and I would never do anything to betray that trust.

So even when I got close enough to the nursery to hear the wailing, I kept walking. I slowed down a little bit, I admit. I might have winced. But I didn't stop.

"I *want* to go to the parade!" That was Baro, who, at five years old, had perfected the art of the tantrum. "It's not fair! Everyone in the whole world gets to do what they want except me!"

A thud, a crash, and another set of wails—these coming from one-year-old Elrin. I quickened my step, which made me trip on a loose section of the rug. I caught myself against the wall and kept going.

"I'm a *prince*! That means I can do whatever I want!"

I broke into a jog and wrenched the nursery door open, just in time to see Baro dump a bottle of purple glitter over his little brother's head.

"Baro!" Gilma cried. "Oh, don't do that!"

Baro grabbed a jar of glue.

"No, no, no." Gilma wrung her hands. "That's not how a prince should behave!"

Elrin yowled, grabbed a chunk of his older brother's hair, and yanked. Baro shrieked.

"Stop fighting!" Gilma wailed. "What would your subjects think?"

I strode into the room, grabbed Elrin's hand, and disentangled it from Baro's hair. Then I held Elrin out of his brother's reach. Glitter rained down from his clothes, covering me with purple sparkles.

"I have a *great* idea," I said. "Once you stop screaming, I'll tell you all about it."

While I was waiting Baro out, I calmed Elrin down by giving him a sweet pop. He nuzzled into my shoulder and sucked happily, drizzling sticky saliva down the side of my neck.

"He shouldn't be having sweets, Tirza," Gilma said.

I gave her a look. She gave me a look right back, then held a hand out to Baro. "Do you want to help me clean up? I'll let you hold the dustpan."

Baro grabbed my skirt and buried his face in it. Gilma's mouth twisted. She went and got a broom and dustpan from the corner.

I thought about offering to help. Gilma, like me, had an odd position at court: She was a village girl who had been hired long ago as a nursemaid, but she was also given gowns and her own room and allowed to attend banquets and balls when the princes were asleep. That had caused a lot of muttering at court, but eventually, everyone had concluded that it was evidence of the queen's sweetness and good nature. After all,

Queen Ella had once been a commoner, too, just like Gilma.

And like me.

So there had been a time—a brief time—when Gilma and I had been close. Cinderella had suddenly become too busy being queen to spend time with me, and Gilma had been like a replacement older sister. But she had quickly realized that it was bad enough being a commoner in fancy clothes without also having the queen's wicked stepsister glued to her side. It hadn't taken her long to join the noblewomen in their whispers and sneers. Then one day, when I was seven years old, she had poured green dye into my hair while two noble girls held me down. They had laughed and laughed. Even more than I remembered the humiliation of walking around with green hair, I remembered the pure delight in Gilma's laugh.

Gilma had been banned from the ball that year, and instead was forced to spend the evening emptying all the castle chamber pots. Ever since then, she had hated me.

By the time Gilma had finished cleaning the glitter (well, most of it—there is glitter in that room to this day), Baro had calmed down. "What's your idea?" he demanded. "Are we going to the parade?"

"Certainly not!" Gilma snapped. "Bad enough that

you keep sneaking into your mother's room. Do you know who gets in trouble when you don't stay where you belong? *I* do, that's who."

Baro's lower lip jutted out, and his eyes welled up with tears.

"I have something better!" I said quickly. I knelt in front of Baro—which, unfortunately, meant I put my knee down in an unnoticed patch of glitter. And this dress was almost new; the laundress was going to hate me even more than she already did. "Do you know how *hot* it is, standing outside in the sun to watch a parade? I would rather be here."

Gilma snorted. "Convenient, since *you're* definitely not allowed to go."

She wasn't wrong, but she also wasn't helping.

"I'm sad to miss the parade too," Gilma went on, stretching her arms above her head. "But at least I have the ball to look forward to, and that's just three nights away. The queen gave me a new gown, and it's absolutely gorgeous. It's too bad you won't get to see it, Tirza."

I kept my eyes on Baro, lowering my voice. "Let's stay here and make an obstacle course."

Tears spilled onto Baro's chubby cheeks. "I hate obstacle courses!"

"Why?"

"I don't know," Baro said. "What's an obstacle course?"

While I explained, Gilma hopped onto the window-sill, straining to get a glimpse of the parade. Which wasn't going to happen; the parade was on the opposite side of the castle. I chose not to explain that to her.

Half an hour later, Gilma *still* hadn't caught on, but at least she stayed out of the way of our obstacle course. She kept her face pressed to the glass, contorting her body to try to see from different angles, muttering, "*Why* do these things never start on time?" and "Did I miss it already? It's your fault for distracting me."

"What," a voice from the doorway demanded, "are you doing?"

Gilma turned so fast that she overbalanced, fell off the windowsill, and landed face-first onto the blanket hammock that Baro had been carefully setting up for the past ten minutes. He stared at his ruined construction, let out an outraged wail, then broke down and sobbed.

Elrin, who was watching me tie ropes across the top of the cradle, blinked. His lower lip trembled.

He burst into a loud, delighted laugh.

Baro grabbed a pillow and threw it at his brother. It missed and hit me instead.

Gilma glared at me as if this were *my* fault.

Meanwhile, the person whose fault it *actually* was

stood in the doorway. He crossed his arms over his chest. "I guess the question should be what *were* you doing?"

"It's an obstacle course." I went to pick up Baro, stepping over a maze of wooden blocks. "Well. It was an obstacle course."

"Whatever you say." Aden raised his bushy eyebrows as he surveyed the room. He was wearing his court clothes, the ones he put on when he was selling cupcakes to the nobility—gray trousers that were a tiny bit too long on him and a white tunic embroidered with gold thread. I guessed that his regular clothes were being washed and that was why he wasn't at the parade. He had only one set of nice clothes, and he couldn't risk getting them dirty.

"It *was* a mess, and now it's an even worse mess," Gilma snapped, glaring at him.

Aden winked at me. "I'm bored. Come to the northern battlements?"

Baro was still wailing into my shoulder—which was now soaked with his tears—and Elrin looked like *he* was going to cry because I had abandoned him. I shook my head.

"What's on the northern battlements?" Gilma demanded.

The answer was an *actual* view of the parade. Of course, Gilma couldn't leave the princes unattended, but what if we took Baro and Elrin with us? Aden would grumble, but the children would love it. It might even make Baro stop crying about his ruined masterpiece. I opened my mouth to suggest it.

"And don't think you can leave me with this mess," Gilma said. "I won't stand for it. You're not actually of royal blood, you know. You may like to forget it, but I assure you, no one else in this castle ever does."

I shut my mouth.

Aden looked from Gilma to me. "Er . . . should I help clean up?"

"Nope," I said. I kissed Baro's smooth cheek and put him down. Glitter scattered off my skirt and rained down on the floor. "I'm sure Gilma can handle all this. Let's go."

———◆———

As we walked through the hallway, I felt a tiny bit guilty for leaving the children behind. But Aden's presence at my side was worth the discomfort. I hadn't seen him for two weeks. And though it wasn't unusual for him to disappear without telling me why, it still made me panic every time. I had spent the past fourteen days wondering if I had done something to make him hate me, or if someone had told him something terrible about me, or if he had just realized that nobody else in the castle understood why he spent so much time with me.

If he had finally realized I wasn't worth it.

I couldn't have blamed him if he had. When Aden wasn't around, it was glaringly obvious how much everyone else in the castle disliked me. Nobody was outright mean to me, not since Gilma's punishment after the hair incident. But they didn't meet my eyes; they spoke to me only as much as was strictly necessary; and they certainly never, ever invited me to do anything with them.

I knew I was supposed to be grateful that Gilma had been punished—like I was supposed to be grateful for everything the queen did for me. But it had made my life a million times harder. The other girls didn't dare touch me anymore, but they made up for it with sly jeers and caustic laughs, a hundred tiny cuts a day. They never let up, and they never would.

If Queen Ella had asked for my advice back then, I would have told her to leave Gilma alone. But she hadn't asked. Gilma's punishment, after all, had impressed everyone with how fair and gracious the queen was. So what if it made everything worse for me?

Everyone in the castle liked *Aden*, though. The commoners joked and laughed with him, and the nobles eagerly purchased the cupcakes he brought in from the village. He was always welcome to join any group in the castle . . . as long as he didn't drag me along.

Every once in a while he took a break from being friends with me. Every time, I was terrified that he had finally given up on me, and every time, I accepted his return gratefully. But this morning, I had come to realize that I was being selfish.

"You know," I said, and my voice caught. I cleared my throat and started again. "You don't have to be my friend."

"Of course I don't have to," Aden said. He was a few steps ahead of me, and he didn't slow down. "I like you."

"Then why have you been ignoring me?"

He hesitated—just for a second, but I knew him well enough to catch it. "I haven't been. . . ."

I rushed to catch up with him, got my feet tangled together, and caught myself against the wall. Aden turned, held out a hand as if to help me, but then dropped it to his side.

"I was feeling guilty," he muttered. "I'm sorry."

"Guilty for what?"

"For nothing," he said forcefully. "I don't have anything to feel guilty about. I just got confused." He turned away. "Come on. If we don't hurry, we'll miss the parade."

He took off at a near run.

Looking back . . . If only I had stopped him. If only I had pressed him and forced him to explain.

It probably wouldn't have made a difference. That's what I tell myself now, anyway.

But we'll never know because I didn't say anything. I was relieved to be done with that conversation. So I followed him, without the slightest idea of what a terrible mistake I was making.

About the Author

Leah Cypess is the author of *Thornwood* and *Glass Slippers*, the first two books in the Sisters Ever After series. She lives in the kingdom of Silver Spring, Maryland, with her family and knows to never, ever make a bargain she can't keep.

leahcypess.com